Cool fingers touched her shoulder.

Merri's eyelids opened and she sat up from the tub, crossing her arms to cover herself.

Brandon Thomas stood next to the tub. His bare chest immediately captured Merri's attention. Wide shoulders, lean waist and lots of muscled terrain in between. The jeans hung low on his hips, giving just a glimpse of the dark, silky hair that vee'd down to off-limits territory.

"Is something wrong?" She really didn't know what else to say.

"The house phone is ringing off the hook." He planted his hands on those lean hips. "Didn't you hear it?"

She twisted the faucet knobs to the off position then flashed him a proper glare. "I guess not." Her chin shot up a little as defiance arrowed through her. "The water was running and the door was closed."

"What do you want me to do?"

Climb in here with me crossed her mind. But this was definitely not the time, much less the place.

His dark, dark eyes connected with hers then and what she saw startled her. Approval. He liked what he saw.

DEBRA WEBB

FIRST NIGHT

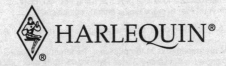

HARLEQUIN®

TORONTO • NEW YORK • LONDON
AMSTERDAM • PARIS • SYDNEY • HAMBURG
STOCKHOLM • ATHENS • TOKYO • MILAN • MADRID
PRAGUE • WARSAW • BUDAPEST • AUCKLAND

This story is dedicated to all the loyal fans
who couldn't wait to read the next story
featuring Merrilee Walters of Silhouette Bombshell's
SILENT WEAPON and SILENT RECKONING.

Recycling programs
for this product may
not exist in your area.

ISBN-13: 978-0-373-88947-1

FIRST NIGHT

ABOUT THE AUTHOR

Debra Webb was born in Scottsboro, Alabama, to parents who taught her that anything is possible if you want it bad enough. She began writing at age nine. Eventually, she met and married the man of her dreams, and tried some other occupations, including selling vacuum cleaners, working in a factory, a day-care center, a hospital and a department store. When her husband joined the military, they moved to Berlin, Germany, and Debra became a secretary in the commanding general's office. By 1985 they were back in the States, and finally moved to Tennessee, to a small town where everyone knows everyone else. With the support of her husband and two beautiful daughters, Debra took up writing again, looking to mysteries and movies for inspiration. In 1998, her dream of writing for Harlequin Books came true. You can write to Debra with your comments at P.O. Box 64, Huntland, Tennessee 37345, or visit her Web site at www.debrawebb.com to find out exciting news about her next book.

Books by Debra Webb

HARLEQUIN INTRIGUE

934—THE HIDDEN HEIR*
951—A COLBY CHRISTMAS*
983—A SOLDIER'S OATH†
989—HOSTAGE SITUATION†
995—COLBY VS. COLBY†
1023—COLBY REBUILT*
1042—GUARDIAN ANGEL*
1071—IDENTITY UNKNOWN*
1092—MOTIVE: SECRET BABY
1108—SECRETS IN FOUR CORNERS
1145—SMALL-TOWN SECRETS††
1151—THE BRIDE'S SECRETS††
1157—HIS SECRET LIFE††
1173—FIRST NIGHT*

*Colby Agency
†The Equalizers
††Colby Agency: Elite Reconnaissance Division

CAST OF CHARACTERS

Merrilee Walters—The newest investigator on staff at the Colby Agency. Merri fights hard to prove she's got what it takes despite being deaf.

Brandon Thomas—He's the prime suspect in his roommate's murder. Can he prove he didn't kill the man with whom he had a volatile relationship?

Victoria Colby-Camp—The head of the Colby Agency.

Ian Michaels—One of Victoria's seconds in command. He has misgivings around Merri, particularly when the case involves a man who obviously has a challenge of his own.

Simon Ruhl—The other second in command at the Colby Agency. Simon is certain Merri is capable and ready. But will his confidence be shaken when, more than once, she barely escapes death?

Kevin "Kick" Randolph—What was he working on that got him killed?

Clive Mathis—The head of Chicago's Crime Commission wants this case solved ASAP without the wrong kind of interference or press coverage.

Homicide Detective Whitehall—He's in charge of solving this case. Mathias is breathing down his neck. He believes he doesn't need the Colby Agency's kind of help.

Bethany Stover—Kick's sister may hold the key to the secret that got him killed. Will that knowledge cost her life, as well?

Lester and Karen Randolph—Will Kick's parents become targets, too?

Chapter One

Friday, Dec. 23, 5:45 p.m.

Merrilee Walters shut down her computer and sighed. Her first report as an assistant field investigator was complete. She smiled. She was a full-fledged Colby Agency investigator now.

Merri slid back her chair and stood. She'd proven to Ian Michaels, the second-in-command here at the Colby Agency, that she could pull her weight despite her disability. Ian was still dubious, hence the continued insistence that for a time Merri would be teamed with another investigator on a case. Getting past that final test would be a breeze.

Pulling on her coat, she considered the seven years that had passed since she'd lost her ability to hear. Life had been tough at first. Being a grown woman and an elementary schoolteacher at the time, she'd had to work particularly hard to regain her bearings. She'd taken a year off from work to adjust to this new soundless world of hers and during that time she'd realized that returning to the world of teaching wasn't possible.

Not for her, anyway.

She'd also realized during that time that she had not lived up to her expecta-tions—expectations she hadn't even realized she'd had at the time.

Merri grabbed her purse and shook her head as she recalled those confusing months. She'd lacked the confidence necessary to have a classroom full of ele-mentary students depending upon her when she couldn't hear a single word or sound. Anything could have happened when she had her back turned, to write on the blackboard for instance. But there had been *more* missing.

Her family had been worried. Her country singer fiancé had broken off their engagement.

Life had pretty much sucked.

Until she'd realized, sort of by trial and error, her true calling. Another smile tugged at her lips. She'd come a long way since then.

Merri turned off the light and stepped out of her office. A stint with Nashville's Metro Police Department had provided the challenge she'd needed and the opportunity to prove she was still a viable member of society. Not to mention she'd had a hell of an adventure.

Four years as a detective back in Nashville had been good, but she'd needed a change. She'd needed to do something more, something much more personal. Victoria Colby-Camp had been willing to take her on and Merri had made a move north, leaving behind the two men who'd turned her world upside down—Detective Steven Barlow and former Mob wiseguy Mason Conrad.

Talk about covering both ends of the spectrum.

Merri had needed a change, professionally and personally. No offense to her colleagues, and certainly not to her family.

She paused in the lobby to peer out the window at the falling snow. She liked Chicago. It was a lot colder than in Nashville and her folks were seriously missing her, but the change had been a good one. One she'd needed on every level.

The rest of the agency staff had gone home for the day. There were last-minute Christmas shopping and holiday parties. But Merri had already done her shopping. Presents to her family had gone into the mail last week. She didn't know enough folks to be invited to any parties, except for the Colby Agency New Year's party. But that was okay. Merri was still getting her Yankee legs under her. And she felt comfortable with being all by herself on Christmas.

If she had gone home, her family would have spent the entire holiday explaining how she needed to come back home to them. One or more of her former colleagues would have dropped by to say how sorely she was missed.

Maybe next year. Right now, she needed distance…distance and time.

She pressed the call button for the elevator and considered what she should have for dinner on the way home. It was actually cheaper for one to eat out and the restaurant crowd prevented her from eating alone, which was something she, as much as she hated to admit it, missed about being back home. Her close-knit family liked nothing better than to get together over a big meal—no special occasion needed.

The elevator light for her floor blinked and the doors prepared to glide open.

"Finally." One would think that with most everyone in the building gone for the day that the elevators would be ready instantly. Never happened. The elegant cars had one speed—*slow*.

The doors slid apart and Merri prepared to move forward.

A blur of movement had her stumbling back several steps.

"You have to…me."

Merri blinked, stared at the man's face. He'd said something but, distracted by his unexpected burst from the car, she'd missed part of it.

"Excuse me?" She kept her attention fully on the man's face this time.

"I need help."

His frantic expression and the fear in his eyes told her he was in trouble. "What's wrong?" She should have just told him they were closed, but she couldn't bring herself to ignore a person in need and this gentleman was definitely in serious need.

The question of how he got past security briefly crossed her mind. But it was the night before Christmas Eve, and it was only minutes before six. Security was likely on rounds. All entrances were secured at six o'clock. A lapse in vigilance could be expected under the circumstances.

The man in front of her shook his head. "I am… my roommate was murdered and…" His head started that fierce wagging again that prevented her from a descent view of his lips.

It was then that Merri noticed the blood-splattered on his T-shirt and the fact that he wasn't wearing a coat. It was freezing outside. Snowing! He had to be nuts! Or drug-crazed.

Merri's instincts shot into survival mode. Her right hand slid into her purse, her fingers going automatically around the canister of pepper spray. "Let's start with what happened." She gestured to his blood-splattered T-shirt with her free hand.

He looked down at himself, shuddered and then shook his head a third time. "My roommate was…back at my…"

This simply wasn't going to work. Merri waved a hand in front of his face to get his full attention. "Look at me when you speak, please."

A frown furrowed his brow. Dark brown tendrils of hair fell around his face. His hair was a little long and unkempt, as if he hadn't combed it today. And his eyes—they were so dark brown they were almost black. She blinked, surprised that she'd gotten that hung up that quickly with his eyes.

"What?" he asked, the demand etched in frustration across his brow.

"Why is there blood on your shirt and where's your coat?" She wasn't going to mention her inability to hear until absolutely necessary. This man had appar-

ently come to the Colby Agency looking for help. She was the only one here,
that left determining a course of action
up to her. She consciously steadied her
breathing in order to slow her heart and
to keep the panic in check. She was a
professional. A full-fledged investigator. She could handle this. Whatever *this*
was.

As requested, he directed his full attention to her face and said, "My roommate
was murdered early this morning. I evidently slept through whatever happened.
When I woke up and discovered his...
him, I called 911. The police hauled me
in. I didn't get a chance to get my coat."
He shrugged as if he didn't know what
else she wanted him to say.

He was wearing lounge pants, she
realized. And flip-flops. Damn. His feet
had to be freezing. It was a long walk
from the nearest precinct to here. And
since she didn't see a pocket for his
wallet, he'd likely been without the funds

for a cab. "So," she surmised, "you've just come from the police?"

He nodded. "They didn't arrest me, but they said I was a person of interest or—" he looked at the floor, shook his head again "—is crazy. I didn't do anything. I wouldn't kill anyone. Not even my roommate who was a complete jerk most of the time, but he was my best friend." Those dark eyebrows drew together. "He's dead."

Though she'd missed part of his words, she got the point. She considered taking him to her office, but that probably wasn't such a good idea since she was here alone. She should call Ian or Simon. Simon Ruhl was another of Victoria's seconds-in-command. He'd been really nice to Merri from the beginning. He believed in her and she appreciated that more than words could say.

Okay. Do this right, Merri.

First step, get the client at ease.

"I'm Merri Walters," she said, "What's your name?"

"Brandon Thomas."

"Well—" she gestured to a chair with her free hand "—Brandon, have a seat." Her fingers released the canister and she dragged a notepad and pen from her purse. She crossed to the receptionist's desk and leaned a hip against it, then prepared to take notes. "Let's start back at the beginning and you tell me exactly what happened. Every detail."

She had to remind him a time or two to look at her when he spoke. Most folks believed she was measuring whether they were telling the truth when she did this. Since he didn't ask why, she supposed he assumed the same. According to his statement, he'd awakened at six and discovered his roommate dead in the living room. After determining that he could not help his friend, he'd called the police. But they weren't buying his story, particularly since some of the neighbors had reported that he and his roommate, Kick Randolph, had an intensely volatile relationship. The roommate apparently owed Brandon a considerable sum of money. All in all, there was plenty of motive and no other suspects. The police had every reason to treat him as a person of interest.

Brandon threaded his fingers through his thick, dark hair. "Look, I don't know who killed him, but—" he looked straight into Merri's eyes "—Kick was into something. He was scared the last couple of days. The police won't believe me, but I'm telling you it had something to do with this CIA-type guy he'd covertly met with on several occasions."

"Can you be more specific about the man?" A CIA-type guy was a pretty broad description. Probably an analogy he made from the movies he'd seen. "Do you know the man's name or where he works?"

Brandon gave another of those adamant shakes of his head. "I only saw him once, and that was at night from across the street. Dark hair." He shrugged. "Medium height and build."

"What gave you the impression he worked for the CIA?" Merri understood the stereotype he meant, but she needed his interpretation.

"You know. Trench coat. Fedora. Starched trousers. The whole federal agent style. Like you see in the movies."

That was what she'd thought. She inclined her head and considered what he'd told her. "You said the man had dark hair. Did he have dark hair or did he wear a dark hat?" From a distance it would be difficult to distinguish one from the other, particularly at night.

Brandon blinked as if he didn't understand the question. "I…I think it was his hair. Maybe he wasn't wearing a hat."

"But you're sure you saw him at night…from across the street?" They needed to get the facts straight. No guessing.

"Definitely at night." Brandon nodded. "I was going into the building. We live in one of the old duplexes off the South Loop. The front stoop is fairly close to the street. He and Kick were having an argument outside his car. I heard their raised voices, but I can't remember precisely what they were talking about."

"What did his car look like?" A tag number would be good.

"Dark. Blue or black. Four doors…I think. Not American, I don't believe."

If this was any indication of the kind of information he gave the police, it was no wonder they considered him a suspect. He contradicted himself almost as often as he concluded with any certainty.

"You didn't see the license plate? Illinois tag or another state?"

He moved his head side to side. "The car was parallel parked. All I saw was Kick arguing with him next to the passenger side of the car."

"You weren't close enough to make an estimation of the man's age?"

"No."

"To some degree, your roommate confided in you as to his dealings with this man. You said the meetings were covert."

Brandon nodded. "Kick said the meetings were very secretive."

"Was he working for this man? Running errands? Can you give me an idea on the nature of the business? Was your roommate gainfully employed?"

"Kick is…was a junior reporter over at the *Trib*. But he said he had the proof he needed to write the kind of story that would put him on top in the investigative journalist field. He wanted his own byline. Problem was, the other guy—the one he argued with—wanted the proof, too. He said it was Kick's civic duty to turn the evidence over to him. Kick refused."

"You don't have any idea what this evidence was or against whom it proved significant?"

"I know it was some kind of video… but I don't know what it was about or who it involved."

"Did he talk to anyone at work regarding this big story he was working?" Perhaps one of his co-workers wanted this big story badly enough to kill for it.

"No way." Brandon finally reclined in his chair, as if he'd relaxed to some degree. "Kick said he couldn't risk telling a soul or they would steal it. He couldn't tell anyone exactly what was going on. Not even me."

Merri could understand the dead man's doggedness and uncertainty about sharing. She'd been digging around in a cold case for days before anyone found out. Been there, done that. Problem was, she could have gotten herself killed… just like this potential client's roommate had quite possibly done.

She summoned her determination. The Colby Agency prided itself on solving the most puzzling cases. If Brandon was being straight with her, then he had plenty of reason to worry and very few pieces of what could only be called a bizarre puzzle. "All right, then." Merri closed her notepad, shoved it and the pen into her purse. "We'll just have to determine the nature of the story your roommate was working on and uncover the identity of this man with whom he exchanged heated words."

The fear and frustration laid claim to Brandon's face once more. "Kick kept his files hidden. What he was working on, the notes, the video, all of it could be anywhere. That man could have the story by now, for all I know. He may have killed my roommate for the information he needed." He blinked. "But what if we can't find him?"

"That's a strong possibility." Merri couldn't speculate just yet exactly what steps they would take if the only other known suspect was beyond their reach. "But," she went on, "whether we find him or not, our top priority will be proving your innocence. It's possible that the forensic evidence will do that for us. It's too early to know that yet. If the police had solid evidence linking you to the murder, you would have remained in custody. Cutting you loose means they aren't sure just how you fit into the equation yet."

There was one other thing he needed to be made aware of. "There is a possibility that if this man is concerned that you saw him, even from across the street, he may consider you a threat. If he, in fact, killed your roommate, he may decide it's in his best interests to tie up any loose ends."

"That's what I tried to tell the police." Brandon rocketed to his feet. "They questioned me for hours." His jaw hardened visibly. "I think they wanted me to confess or something. But I didn't do it."

Merri felt for the guy. "Since you don't have an alibi, we'll need to find someone who can vouch for your character enough to convince the police that you wouldn't commit such a heinous crime. Or," she offered, "we'll have to find evidence that proves, in addition to having had access to your roommate, someone, like the man you saw, had an equally strong motive for wanting to kill him. Before we can do that, we have to determine what your roommate was working on."

Brandon looked at her as if he'd just experienced an epiphany. "If the evidence hasn't been taken, I have the means to locate it."

Hold on. "You have proof of what you're saying? Then why didn't you give this proof to the police?" That would have made his life immensely less complicated the last several hours. He wouldn't have had to come here. She would already be having dinner at a fine restaurant.

Brandon bit the inside of his jaw as if he

were considering a logical response. "I can't remember the riddle…the clues." He closed his eyes and shook his head. "I did tell the police but when I couldn't produce the proof, they assumed I was lying."

His face said that he desperately wished he hadn't had to tell her that last part. For the first time in a very long time, Merri wished she could hear the inflection in his voice. The little nuances that gave meaning to one's words. But she couldn't. So she had no choice but to rely on her instincts. And her instincts were screaming at her that something was very wrong with this guy and/or his story.

Maybe not with him personally, but with the sequence of events or with his reasoning. She couldn't quite put her finger on the problem, but the teacher side of her—the one that sized up kids in a heartbeat—was sounding that too familiar alarm.

"What do you mean, you don't remember the riddle or clues?" The first stirrings of fear awakened in her belly. She was well aware that drug addiction created memory lapses. She surveyed her would-be client once more. To say he fit the profile would be an understatement. But she knew from experience that first impressions were not always fair. She needed more.

"I told you that Kick kept everything hidden so no one could steal his work?"

She nodded, though she wasn't sure where he was headed with this or why he felt compelled to ask the question. Could he not remember what he'd said to her two minutes ago? Her right hand slid automatically back to her purse.

"He didn't trust a safe or jump drive or any damn thing." Brandon's forehead lined with his determined concentration. "Once when he was drunk he gave me this ridiculous riddle and explained that he kept the important stuff hidden that way. The riddle had clues to the location. I couldn't get it right for the police. They had cops checking all the wrong places." His chest heaved with a big breath. "I ended up looking like a fool and as guilty as hell."

Merri had an idea. She had used it with her students all the time. Maybe she was crazy, but she had nothing more exciting to do tonight. Her appetite had vanished in the wake of the adrenaline coursing through her veins. Truth be told, she wasn't afraid of this guy, despite the blood on his clothes.

"Do you recall how long ago it was that Kick told you this riddle?"

Another of those halfhearted male shrugs. "Couple months ago, maybe. Not all that long ago."

"Where were you when the two of you had this conversation?"

"The apartment. Drinking cold ones. Watching a game." Another shrug. "That's what we did most of the time since he was always broke. His need to sink all his earnings into the tools of his trade was an ever-present sore spot between us. I didn't like paying his share of the rent along with mine."

Merri made up her mind. "Let's take a look at your apartment."

Yeah, she probably was crazy.

But this was her case.

And she might be deaf, but she wasn't blind. If this guy made one wrong move, he would be begging for the police to pick him up again. She was well-trained and knew how to protect herself.

If her plan didn't work, she would call Simon for backup. She headed for the elevators, her client followed. When she turned back to him, he stabbed the call button for the elevator and said, "Thank you."

As the doors glided open behind him, Merri searched his eyes. "For what?"

"For taking a chance on a guy like me. That doesn't happen real often."

Chapter Two

7:58 p.m.

The apartment was in an old building off the South Loop that lacked the care and restoration of some in the neighborhood. There was no elevator, so that meant climbing the stairs to the third floor. Ancient graffiti covered the stairwell walls. The tile floors were worn. The doors looked secure, but the place smelled of neglect. If Brandon had said anything to Merri on the way up the stairs, she missed it. Since he didn't look back at her in question, she assumed he hadn't.

She'd noticed him shiver once or twice. He had to be freezing, especially his feet in those flip-flops.

Brandon paused at the door marked 11 and looked at her for advice on proceeding. Two strips of official yellow crime scene tape had been placed across the center of the door, along with a proclamation declaring the premises off limits to anyone but official police personnel.

If, as he'd said, Brandon had been questioned for hours, chances were the forensics techs had come and gone already. The scene wouldn't likely be released until the detective in charge determined that there was nothing else to be gained by maintaining the off-limits edict. All that meant, in her opinion, was that they shouldn't touch anything that might be evidence.

Been there, done that, too. Merri wasn't exactly concerned about bending that particular rule. She knew her way around a crime scene. Holding out her hand, Brandon placed the key there. She unlocked and opened the door, then ducked beneath the warning tape. If Simon had been here he would have called someone, a Colby connection with Chicago PD, to get permission. But Simon wasn't here. As long as Merri was careful and didn't prompt any serious repercussions for the agency, all would be okay.

She could do this.

After closing the door behind Brandon, she locked it to be sure no one else was tempted to try the same approach.

"Don't touch anything unless it's absolutely essential. And watch your step." She glanced pointedly at the blood-stained carpet and official signs of where the body had been discovered.

He nodded, his attention lingering on the place where he'd found his roommate early that morning.

With a long, slow perusal around the room, Merri decided the apartment was the typical bachelor pad. Not neat by any stretch of the imagination, particularly after the tossing the forensics techs had done in their search for evidence. The signs that prints had been lifted dusted most surfaces—not that there were that many pieces of furniture. A futon for a sofa, a television and a long, narrow coffee table were the only furnishings aside from a desk with its mountains of computer equipment and a drawing desk with much the same. The roommate clearly had had a serious compulsion when it came to technology. Merri hadn't once seen a setup like this outside a major tech center.

"Wow."

Brandon said, "Yeah I know. Kick didn't take any shortcuts when it came to having the latest and greatest in hardware and software. It was just his share of the rent and basic essentials for survival that he had trouble coughing up."

Merri considered the statement. "Is

that why the two of you had what your neighbors termed a *volatile* relationship?"

"Mostly." Brandon glanced around his disheveled living space. "Kick didn't see this environment as permanent. He was a dreamer. Had big plans."

Whereas Brandon was a realist. That part she got. "Let's talk about the proof you mentioned." The fact that he couldn't remember exactly where that proof was didn't offer much security in the way of proving his innocence. Seemed to her that the police, given enough digging, would find some trace on the two or three hard drives of what the victim had been up to. The Feds certainly knew how to discover the unfindable when it came to digital footprints. The Colby Agency too had analysts for just that sort of investigation.

"No one will find anything related to the big story on his computer," Brandon observed when her gaze settled on his face once more.

"How can you be so sure?" No matter that his roommate obviously had bragged about maintaining a high level of security, new ways to find digital traces were discovered every day. Few could proclaim exception to that ever-changing investigative technology. But many tried. "If he worked on his equipment in any capacity, a digital trail was left behind. Even if he meticulously wiped his hard drive. There are those who know how to resurrect the smallest detail."

"No one was more aware of that vulnerability," Brandon explained. "Kick did his secret work someplace else." Brandon walked over to the desk with its mountain of hardware and monitors. The dramatic waving of his arms told her he'd said something about all the stuff there but he hadn't been looking at her so she had no idea what came out of his mouth.

When he turned to her in question, she asked, "What do you mean?" That prompt usually worked at garnering a repeat of a statement.

Brandon plopped down in the swivel chair next to the desk. "He did everything right here as long as it wasn't related to *the* story. *That* he did someplace else. The police won't find what they're looking for here."

And that was what he'd tried to explain when questioned. Merri risked turning her back on him—which meant she wouldn't know if he said anything—and wandered through the rest of the two-bedroom, one-bath apartment. The two bedrooms were furnished in an equally Spartan manner. A bed, nightstand and dresser stood in each. No curtains, just the blinds that had likely been there a few decades. The closets had been ransacked for evidence. Mounds of clothes and other stuff had been piled on the bed.

The kitchen was tiny, with only the essentials. Two days' worth of eating utensils cluttered the sink.

When she returned to the living room, Brandon still sat in the chair at the computer desk. The telephone nearby served as the base, with two satellite handsets, one in each bedroom. The red light that indicated the answering machine was set to record incoming calls wasn't blinking. No messages. If there had been anything relevant on the phone, the police would have taken it.

Her new client hadn't attempted to follow her around the apartment and simply stared at her in question when she returned. That assured her that he hadn't asked or said anything she had missed.

"How long have you lived here?" Surely a man who put down roots for an extended period would have decorated to some degree. The quilt with all the little flowers that covered the bed in Brandon's room didn't count. A mother or grandmother had likely given that to him in an effort to ensure he didn't freeze. Either one would likely be mortified by his leaving home this close to Christmas wearing nothing but flip-flops. Not to mention the blood-splattered T-shirt.

"Three years." Brandon braced his forearms on his spread knees. "Kick moved in about six months after me. He responded to an ad for a roommate I placed in the classifieds. We became close friends over the past two and a half years."

The idea of just how much time the two had spent here gave new meaning to living sparsely. "Okay." Deciding not to shrug off her coat, Merri took a seat on the futon-style sofa facing her client. "Let's talk about the time when Kick told you about how he hid his big story."

Brandon straightened from his relaxed position immediately. He sat up straight and blinked. Merri gave him sufficient time to think about her prompt. Still, he hesitated, allowing the minutes to drag by. The confusion in his gaze and the lined expression of concentration on his face told her he was struggling with a response. The suggestion hadn't been that complicated.

She'd watched the kids in her class do this plenty of times. But Brandon Thomas was no kid. That he took so long to finally attempt an answer had dread trickling through her. If he had planned to lie, he'd have come up with something to say a lot faster. The truth should have come nearly as quickly as a manufactured statement.

Delayed reaction. That could point to a number of problems. She needed more insight into this guy.

"Was it nighttime or daytime?" she prompted.

He blinked. "Night."

Good. "You said he was drinking? Were you drinking?" That could very well be the underlying problem with his slow responses to her questions.

He started to nod, but then shook his

head. "I don't really drink. Not…" His shoulders rose and fell in one of those shrugs that typically indicated indifference, but she had a feeling the action was more about hesitation for him. He was filling the time until he decided what to say next. "Not really."

She rephrased the question. "So you weren't drinking that night?"

"Maybe a beer or two." He searched her eyes a moment then dropped his head.

"Brandon."

He lifted his gaze back to hers.

"A beer or two is all?" She'd learned numerous techniques for getting around the warning that he must look at her when he spoke. She'd said that a couple of times already. Restating the warning would only raise his suspicions.

"I mostly nurse a drink. Just…to fit in. You know, socially."

That she understood. She did it too often to admit. Most folks, especially

Merri, resented admitting his or her challenges. "Then you clearly recall that he specifically mentioned keeping this story—the one the man you can't identify was interested in preventing him from pursuing—hidden where no one could possibly find it."

"Yes."

"What portion of the riddle do you remember?"

"On the range." He concentrated long and hard. Several seconds. "Nothing can change. My space and no place. Invisible."

"You're sure that's exactly what he said and how he said it?" Merri pulled her notepad and pen from her purse and wrote down the words. Range could mean stove or cook top. His space could mean where he lives or works. No place? Nothing came to mind...except that she could see why the police had no idea what the hell any of it meant. She guessed Brandon's statement regarding the so-called puzzle was being run through the Bureau's ciphers to determine if it was some sort of code.

Then again, perhaps she was reading far too much into this case. Kick Randolph wasn't a high-level reporter. He was just a junior wannabe. Did the police really have any reason to extend any extra effort to solve his homicide? As much as she despised the idea, the wealthier or more high-profile the victim, the more time spent on the investigation. Considering the deceased was basically a nobody, chances were this case would end up one of two places—closed, with charges pressed against Brandon, or shoved into a cold case file.

"Maybe. I might not be remembering it correctly."

Those big dark eyes were filled with frustration and defeat. "Brandon, are you on any medication?" A guy who hadn't been drinking and wasn't on any sort of medication shouldn't act so frustrated if he simply couldn't recall the statements made by someone else. Distraction, a busy schedule, any number of excuses could explain his inability to recall the details of that night. Why not say as much rather than becoming more frustrated?

Extreme frustration. Another indicator of an underlying problem.

"No." He looked put out that she'd asked.

"Let's try something else." Another tactic she'd used with her students. "We'll try writing down the dialogue. Sometimes when you look at the written words you remember something you otherwise wouldn't."

He twisted in the chair and picked up a spiral notebook from the desk along with a pen.

"Write what you remember about that evening. Anything at all. Take your time," she assured him when uncertainty claimed his face.

As he focused on the page, she observed

his ability to put his thoughts down in written form, not the writing itself, but the brain-to-fingers interaction. Slow, methodical and intensely thought-out.

Calling Simon Ruhl crossed her mind again. Not yet. She wasn't completely sure there was reason to call at this point. What would she say? *I'm sitting in the apartment of a man splattered in blood. His roommate is dead. The police consider him a suspect but I don't think he did it.*

She would definitely wait about that call.

Minutes ticked by. Three…five…then ten. Finally his fingers flattened the pen against the paper and his attention returned to her. "Done."

Now for the real test. The classic symptoms were undeniable. But Brandon Thomas had to be around thirty years old. No question. Her assessment was not in keeping with his age. He was at least half a decade beyond the usual age guidelines.

"Would you read what you've written to me, please?"

He blinked. Stared at her as if she'd asked him to light himself on fire, then he extended the notebook in her direction. "You read it."

"I need you to read it," she pressed. "Stand up and read it." She hated to add the "stand up" part but if he stood, she would be able to read his lips most of the time from her position below him.

The hesitation lasted at least half a minute. She had almost decided he wasn't going to comply. Finally he stood. As he stumbled through the passage he'd written, he glanced up at her periodically. It wasn't imperative that she catch every word, only that she could see the pacing and flow of how he formed the sentences.

Slow. Halting. As if he had a difficult time reading his own words aloud.

When he'd finished, she held out her hand for the notebook. He placed it in her outstretched palm, his expression full of guilt. He was embarrassed that he couldn't read smoothly. She glanced over what he'd written. His handwriting was bold and neat. But one thing was glaringly apparent. He'd misspelled five words. Two of those words were not only simple but used several times throughout the passage. In each instance, the two words were misspelled differently.

Merri pulled the pages, as well as the three clean ones after the last one, from the notebook, folded and placed them in her purse. She understood Brandon's situation now. As she pushed to her feet, she glanced around the compact living room once more. She would ask him about it… eventually, but not now.

"Why don't you shower and change," she suggested, "and we'll go have coffee some place neutral and try to figure out what Kick was telling you with these seemingly disconnected phrases."

Brandon tugged at the T-shirt he wore, then stood. "You'll…"

He turned away from her as he spoke. But the slumped shoulders told her exactly what he was worried about. "Don't worry. I'll do all I can to help you figure this out, Brandon."

He turned back to her then. "You're sure you're not going to slip out while I'm in the shower?"

What she'd missed was him asking if she would still be here. Made sense in light of the desperation choking his reason and logic. "I won't be going anywhere until we determine how to move forward with proving your innocence. That's a guarantee."

He held her gaze a moment longer. The heavy defeat that had weighed down his shoulders had given way to glittering fear in those dark eyes. Something shifted deep in her chest. She'd only met this guy and already she wanted desperately to help him. There was more here than met the eye, so to speak. Brandon Thomas wouldn't have a chance with the police. If they couldn't find anyone else to hang this one on, they would railroad Brandon or push the case aside.

That he trusted her enough to shower, leaving her to do as she pleased, surprised her and was likely indicative of his desperation. She understood it far better than she wanted to admit.

When the water was going in the bathroom, she carefully went over the apartment once more. Using a pen from her purse, she flipped through files and the desk Rolodex. A framed photograph of Brandon and his roommate showed that the two were about the same age. Both good-looking. Kick's framed degree in journalism decorated the otherwise stark wall above the desk. If Brandon had a degree, he wasn't sporting any indication of the accomplishment. The drawing desk appeared to be where he did his work. After snooping around she decided he was an architect of some sort.

In the deceased's bedroom, she found

several family snapshots in the top drawer of the nightstand. Golf clubs on the bed amid the rest of the items that had been taken from the closet. Kick was not only proud of his accomplishments, he had pricey taste in attire, as well. Designer labels were stamped on virtually all of his sizable wardrobe.

Brandon's bedroom revealed quite the opposite. No family connections that she found. Not a single photo. His closet had apparently been as sparsely furnished as the rest of the apartment. He defined the phrase *living simply*.

It wasn't until she went through the kitchen a second time that she found the shared bulletin board. On the back side of an upper cabinet door was a makeshift bulletin board with numerous handwritten telephone numbers, most belonging to women. Not Brandon's writing. Something else Kick appeared to have plenty of—female attention. Or, at least, their numbers.

Only three names were male, also evidently in Kick's handwriting. Merri made a note of the male names and numbers on one of the sheets she'd tucked into her purse. Though she doubted he would keep the name of the contact Brandon had seen posted in such a way.

The cupboards were bare, as she'd expected. Mismatched dishware and flatware. The dishwasher held nothing but a cup and one small plate; the rest of the soiled eating utensils were in the sink. Microwave and oven were empty. Nothing beneath the stovetop burners. The range in Kick's puzzle definitely wasn't the one in their apartment. Not that she'd expected it would be, but she'd given it a look just the same. She had to cover all bases.

A window above the sink stared directly at another window some twenty feet across a side alley. The neighboring apartment was dark. She wondered briefly if

Brandon ever came face-to-face with his neighbor via this window. A woman would have a shade over that window. She shook her head and leaned down to check the lower-level cabinets.

The cabinet beneath the sink held a few cleaning supplies but nothing else of interest.

The final place she inspected was what at first appeared to be a pantry-type closet but was, in fact, a laundry closet complete with a stackable appliances set. A white button-down shirt had dried in the washer. She wondered why the techs hadn't taken it. As difficult as it had been to see in the white laundry tub, if she'd noticed it, the techs should have. She lifted the stiff material to her face and sniffed. The pungent smell of bleach had permeated the fabric. She shook out the shirt and looked it over, couldn't see any trace of stains.

Merri dropped the shirt back into the washer and leaned forward to see if she could spot anything on either side of the stacked appliances. Nothing but dust bunnies and an old newspaper.

Closing the door, she turned back to the kitchen at large. Her breath trapped in her lungs. Clean shaven, Brandon stood in the doorway. He wore a blue sweater over a white T-shirt, well-worn jeans and the only pair of sneakers she had seen in his room.

"Are you okay?" he asked.

The realization that he'd likely spoken to her once or twice without her reacting was no doubt the reason for the question.

"Is that your shirt?" If she skirted the question smoothly enough he might leave it alone. "The one in the washer?"

He shook his head. "Kick's."

Maybe Kick just liked his whites extra white. That would certainly explain the bleach.

"You ready?" she encouraged, manufacturing a smile of assurance.

"Sure." He glanced around the kitchen

as if he'd just now considered that she had likely looked at everything, hoping to find clues.

Would he worry that she'd found some secret he'd kept? If he was innocent, he had no need to worry. She had already made a preliminary judgment: innocent. That assessment remained subject to change, but she read people fairly well. She picked up no vibes whatsoever that Brandon was the type to hurt another human in this manner. Still, he was guarded.

The hint of suspicion that lingered in his eyes didn't bother her that much. She figured it was as much to do with her lack of a response when he'd entered the room as anything.

"Don't forget your coat." She walked past him and made her way to the front door. There was a coffee shop a few blocks away that would work well for her purposes. She was acquainted with lots and lots of restaurants all over town since she rarely dined at home. The place she had in mind stayed open until eleven, so there was plenty of time. At that point she would decide the best course of action for delving into this case.

After ducking under the tape once more, she waited while Brandon locked the door. His pale blue coat looked lightweight but she knew from the brand, one skiers preferred, that it would keep him warm despite the chilly Chicago weather.

He stood back, allowing her to descend the stairs first. A few steps down, she glanced back to see if he had said anything. That he watched her so closely warned her that he was suspicious to some degree. She would have to share the truth with him—soon.

It was only fair.

She had already made an assessment about his challenges. Approaching the subject would be touchy and would have to wait. Her own challenge, however, would not wait. Yet she put off the inevitable. Selfishly clung to any reprieve. Her previous superior had called her on that strategy many times.

The stairwell abruptly shook as if an earthquake had rocked the entire building or block. Brandon had stopped his downward momentum and now whirled back toward his apartment. With her attention over her shoulder, Merri lost her balance and barely caught the railing before plunging forward.

When the building had stopped shaking, she turned back to check on Brandon and to better assess the situation. The door of his apartment had blown open, and now hung precariously on its hinges. Even as she stared at the unexpected sight, debris drifted downward to settle on the scarred tile floor.

Fear brushed against Merri's skin.

Not an earthquake or any other natural disaster.

An *explosion.*

They had just exited the apartment.

Fifteen, twenty seconds ago! Her sense of smell was keen. She'd noticed no gas…nothing.

Instinct railed at her.

Get out of the building!

Now!

Chapter Three

"Brandon!"

He couldn't look away from the landing outside his door.

"That was an explosion!"

Something had blown up in his apartment! He blinked, stared at the door barely hanging on its hinges.

What the hell had just happened?

"Brandon!"

He turned to the woman waiting a few steps below him. The questions reeling through his mind would be the same as hers. Should they call the police? What the hell would they say? *Your crime scene just blew up.* But this wasn't just a crime scene, this was his home.

"We have to get out of here," Merri urged.

His feet were taking him down the stairs before his brain analyzed her warning. They were in danger. Imminent danger. If they hadn't walked out that door when they had…damn! It was a miracle they weren't dead.

Like Kick.

When Brandon hit the step where she waited, she grabbed his hand and rushed downward. They moved past the second floor and onto the first in record time. He moved toward the front entrance.

She held him back, her face a study in worry. "Is there a rear exit? There could be trouble waiting for us out there."

"A side exit. To the alley."

"We'll try that way."

Once more she urged him forward. He took the lead, showing the way. She stayed close behind him, weaving through the narrow corridor that ended at the only other exit on the ground floor.

Brandon hit the release on the door, bursting out into the alley between his building and the next. The cold air slapped him in the face, making him immensely thankful for the coat and sneakers. He'd half frozen this morning. The cops hadn't cared, probably could care less that there had been an explosion in his apartment, except that there might have been more evidence to collect. This was insane!

Why would anyone do that?

The tug on his hand slowed his rush toward the street. He turned back to the woman who'd stopped shy of his destination.

"We should call the police."

He tried to catch his breath and slow his racing heart. She was right. He patted his pockets for his cell phone. Tried to remember if the police had given the phone back to him. No, he decided, they hadn't, hadn't given him back his wallet, either.

Didn't matter. She had her phone in her hand before he could explain the absence of his own.

Headlights fanned across the dim alley. The vehicle had come from the narrow cross street at the back of the alley. Only the city's garbage collection truck or a delivery truck usually drove through the area. The lights bobbed as the vehicle cut around Dumpsters and trashcans, coming closer. Too close.

What the hell?

She was pulling on his hand again, moving toward the street at the front of the alley.

Hadn't she said they shouldn't go out toward the front?

But the vehicle was bearing down on them now.

After them.

Damn! What the hell?

He surged forward, letting her drag him toward the street.

Tires squealed.

Brandon ran faster in an effort to keep up with the woman one step in front of him.

"Stop!"

The male voice was close behind them. Too close.

Merri Walters kept running for the street that seemed so far away. Brandon slowed but didn't stop as ordered. She kept moving…shouldn't he?

"Stop or I'll shoot!"

Brandon dared to glance back. The blinding headlights on either side of the man made Brandon squint. But there was no mistaking the black ski mask he wore, his fire-ready stance…or the gun in his hand.

Brandon stopped. Merri's forward momentum jerked on his hand. He tightened his grip, halting her movement. He didn't have to wonder if she looked back and saw what he'd seen. She was suddenly standing next to him, staring at the man with the gun.

"Put your hands up," the man warned. "Now!"

Brandon heard the sirens in the distance. Help was on its way, but it wouldn't get here in time to stop this man from shooting one or both of them if they failed to obey his command. Brandon's hands lifted in surrender. Merri looked at him, then did the same. He didn't know if she carried a weapon, but Brandon definitely didn't. This was bad.

"This way," the gunman ordered as he gestured with his weapon toward the van behind him.

Brandon glanced toward the woman at his side. She didn't move. Should he?

"Now!" the man shouted. "Or you're both dead."

Brandon didn't wait for Merri to make the first move. Keeping his hands up, he started toward the van. Merri followed him. Was she playing the part of reluctant victim? Trying to seem the noncompliant of the two? Sort of good cop-bad cop?

The van's side door glided open. Another dark figure popped out. Another weapon. Another mask. What the hell was this? Brandon climbed into what he now recognized as a cargo van. The interior lights were dim, but those from the dash allowed him to see that a network of canvas straps were fashioned like mesh separating the front seats from the open space where Brandon found himself. No seats. The low height of the interior forced him to lower his head and shoulders. His hands remained up as he watched Merri climb into the vehicle.

The gunman behind her shouted, "Sit. Keep your hands on your head." When she didn't readily comply, the man snatched the bag from her shoulder. She glared at him but still did not obey his order. Fear for her safety rammed into Brandon's chest.

The van was moving in reverse before the side door slammed shut. Brandon had scarcely hit the floor, his hands positioned on his head as he'd been told, before the backward momentum had him struggling to stay sitting upright. He resisted the urge to use his hands to keep his balance.

Merri practically fell on top of him as the gunman pushed her to the floor. The first man, the one who'd shouted at them in the alley, was behind the steering wheel. He continued backing the van until he wheeled out onto the cross street at the back of the alley. Brandon got a glimpse of blue lights pulsing from the street at the front of the alley.

The police had arrived…too late for them.

His attention settled on Merrilee Walters. Brandon didn't have to wonder if this had anything to do with Kick's death and his story. Brandon understood that both he and the woman he'd gone to for help were in serious trouble.

The police should have listened to him.

Now they would both likely end up like Kick.

Dead.

MERRI CLOSED HER EYES and ordered them to adjust to the darkness. She had to be able to see the faces and read the lips of anyone speaking. The mask the second gunman wore, like the first, pretty much prevented her from reading his lips. The near nonexistent lighting kept her from seeing Brandon's lips well enough to understand anything he might say.

Brandon leaned slightly closer and whispered something against her ear.

She didn't understand!

She should have told him right up front. That was one of the points Ian Michaels had attempted to get across to her. She could not pretend she was like everyone else. The need to ensure her potential clients understood her lack of hearing was essential.

Ian had been right, it seemed. Simon would be immensely disappointed in her. She'd not only screwed up a case, her actions would likely get both her and the client killed.

Damn it!

Brandon stared at her, his confusion evident in his rigid posture. He had no idea why she chose not to respond to whatever he'd said.

She had messed up.

Maybe her family and Metro's top brass had been right about her. She was handicapped and didn't want to admit her shortcoming. The inability to own her boundaries was a danger to herself and anyone else. The line came up frequently on her performance evaluations.

For years she had fought that issue. Had proven time and again that she could do what any individual who could hear could do.

But she had been wrong. *This* was proof positive.

She watched the gunman standing above them, his fingers locked on an overhead strap to maintain his balance in the moving vehicle.

Brandon elbowed her. She turned toward him. He leaned in, whispered something against her ear yet again. She shuddered, drew away. She didn't dare make eye contact with him until they could speak privately. At this point he would be even more frustrated and confused.

The gunman watching over them released the strap and walked crookedly up to the back of the driver's seat. He glanced at Merri and Brandon before leaning his face closer to the webbing and speaking to the driver.

Brandon was whispering to her again. Damn it! She turned her face to his and whispered, "What?" He attempted to lean close to her ear but she grabbed him by the chin and pointed his face at hers. "Look at me when you speak," she murmured.

Another of those near constant frowns lined his brow. "What do we do now?" he asked, his nose only a few inches from hers.

Her gaze glued to his lips, she got it. "We remain calm," she whispered, "until we learn what this is about." She fixed her eyes directly on his. "No sudden moves. Do exactly as they tell you."

The muzzle of the weapon was suddenly against her head.

Judging by the way Brandon stared up at the gunman, their captor had said something, but Merri hadn't heard his approach or his words.

She looked up at the gunman. Part of her wanted to tell him she was deaf and hope that news would somehow influence his actions. But giving him any usable information would be a mistake.

"Go to hell," she said instead.

The need to grab the overhead strapping to keep his balance prevented the gunman from slapping her but as soon as he had a hold on the strap, he kicked her in the side. The air rushed out of Merri's lungs. She wrapped her arms around her middle, struggled to suck in a breath. Brandon reached for the guy, but she stopped him. Shook her head.

Brandon looked from Merri to the gunman and back. She wished she could see his eyes better. He had to be confused as hell. She'd told Brandon to do whatever they said and she had lashed out.

Dumb move, Merri. But her goal had been accomplished. Whatever the gunman had said to her, she'd covered for her inability to respond appropriately.

Brandon scooted closer, wrapped his arm around her shoulders and pulled her against his chest. The gunman aimed the muzzle at Brandon's face. He stared at it, but didn't make a comment or a move to release his hold on her. The gunman made no further attempt to separate them. She was grateful for that. Somehow she felt safer in Brandon's arms. All this time she'd fought the idea of a protector and here she was…being protected.

Though the gunman grabbed Merri's purse, he hadn't bothered to pat either of them down. Armed or not, the weapon in the bad guy's hand kept them from attempting any escape. The man with the gun was banking on their fear.

Two more times Brandon whispered something to her. Merri turned to him, hoping he would repeat his comments, but he didn't. His continued hold on her gave her an unexpected feeling of strength. She hadn't looked at him that way. But now, with his arm around her shoulders and her upper body supported by his chest, she realized that though he was lean he was well-muscled. Funny, she realized, how first impressions were so many times way off the mark. She told herself that was why she didn't like to explain her hearing challenge when she first met a person. Her shortsightedness regarding Brandon's physical prowess was evidence of that theory. Yet their current situation was serious evidence of the opposite…of hiding her own challenge.

With no windows other than those around the driver's and front passenger's seats, she couldn't assess where they were headed. They'd gone south out of the alley. Since no hard turns had been made she had to assume they were still traveling south. She might not be able to see where they were going but she felt every slowdown and turn. So far they hadn't turned.

As if she'd spoken the observation out loud, the driver slowed and took a hard left. Brandon held her more tightly against him. He smelled good, she realized. No cologne, just the subtle scent

of what was likely his soap or his antiper-
spirant. The urge to close her eyes and
enjoy the secure feeling unexpectedly
overwhelmed her. She mentally shook it
off. What was wrong with her? Yes, it
had been a while since she'd let herself
feel anything in a man's arms. But it
hadn't been that long, had it? Not to
mention this was a stranger. She didn't
often have reactions so strong to strang-
ers.

Another deceleration for a turn sent
her senses on alert. The van didn't speed
up once the turn was made. Merri concluded that they had reached their destination. A hard stop and the change in the
posture of the gunman hovering above
them confirmed her assessment.

The gunman waved his weapon. Merri
understood that he had issued an instruc-
tion but it was totally lost on her.
Brandon released her and scrambled to
his feet. He offered Merri a hand and
she did the same.

The door slid open and the gunman hustled them out. Merri immediately took stock of her surroundings. She blinked to adjust to the bright fluorescent lighting. Large warehouse. The van had driven directly into the warehouse, and the drive-through door had immediately closed. A couple of unopened wooden crates sat against one wall. Another van similar to the one in which they had arrived and a generic four-door black sedan were parked inside. She counted six men, all wearing black from boots to masks. They milled about as if the abducting folks were an everyday affair. To them, it seemed, loading something into the back of the van was paramount. They paid no real attention to the arrival of the hostages. And that was what they were—hostages.

Stop, she ordered herself. *Pay attention to the details.* There was a second floor at the back of the building. Beneath that were several doors leading to what appeared to be offices.

The two masked gunmen who had picked them up led Merri and Brandon to one of the rooms or offices. The room was empty. Once they were shoved inside the door was closed and, Merri presumed, locked. Just in case, she rushed over to the closed door and attempted to open it. Locked. Definitely.

She turned back to Brandon who stood in the middle of the well-lit room staring at her.

"They're going to kill us."

She couldn't argue with his reasoning. "They're going to try." That was a given. Sometime during the run or struggle that followed she had dropped her cell phone. The fact that the 911 dispatcher had been on the line might or might not prove useful. But, as soon as the Colby Agency was contacted, and they would be contacted, that would be a step in the right direction. The agency would pull out all the stops to find her.

"We have to…"

Merri waved to him. "What?" That he'd turned around in a circle and thrust his arms up when he spoke had prevented her from getting all that he said.

He shifted to face her more fully. "Don't you get it? These guys have guns. Do you have a gun?"

"No." She had a weapon at home. But unless she was on assignment, she wasn't supposed to carry it. She wasn't supposed to be on assignment. She wasn't supposed to have a client. She wasn't supposed to allow a client, if she had one, to believe she had no physical challenge. She was batting a thousand on all counts.

"I came to your agency for help." He turned to pace. "And I got…"

Okay, time to tell him.

Merri swallowed back the lump rising in her throat. She hated this part. "Brandon."

He just kept pacing and rambling about something. She could see his lips moving but not from a view that allowed her to understand every word. She could imagine, however, that whatever he was saying about her wasn't particularly flattering.

"Brandon!"

He turned, glared at her.

"There's something I should have told you." The blood pounded in her skull. If she hadn't lost her hearing, the whooshing sound inside her right now would be overwhelming. She braced herself, looked him in the eye and prepared to confess her disability.

Disability.

The word. She hated that word.

"What?" He motioned for her to spit it out.

Just do it, Merrilee.

"Brandon, I—"

That he was staring beyond her now and his eyes had widened with worry warned that someone had walked into the room. She turned around. A man, his mask shielding his face, slammed the door behind him.

Merri focused her gaze on his lips, or what she could see of them. The mask was a little close around his mouth but the bright light helped her to distinguish between the two.

"Against the wall," the man ordered. The pistol in his right hand was leveled on them.

Merri backed across the room, never taking her eyes off the man with the weapon.

When her back hit the wall, she demanded, "What do you want?"

The man glanced at Brandon. "He knows what I want."

Merri assessed the size of the man with the gun. Too tall and heavy to be the one Brandon had seen meeting with his roommate. It appeared to be their original abductor, the one in the alley. Merri turned her face toward Brandon. He was shaking his head and saying something.

The best she could tell it was that he didn't know what the man was talking about.

The muzzle of the weapon suddenly bored into the soft underside of Merri's chin. The man's face was close to hers but she didn't miss all that he said to Brandon. "You'll cooperate or…"

She didn't have to see the movement of his lips to know he'd threatened her life. If she'd had any doubts about what had been said, the terror on Brandon's face told her all she needed to know.

"What is it you think I can help you with?" Brandon asked.

Merri shifted her gaze to the man in front of her. Her heart threatened to burst from her chest. She blocked out the pain caused by the muzzle.

"I want the video."

Video? Had Brandon's roommate actually had an incriminating video? Brandon had mentioned a video. Merri supposed it was related to the story somehow.

"I don't know what you're talking about," Brandon said at last.

Strangely, Merri felt relieved that he hadn't lied to her. Not even by omission. He evidently knew nothing of any video. Other than the bizarre clues he'd shared with her.

"By the time I get through with your girlfriend here," the masked man warned, "you'll remember everything I need to know."

With her head immobile, Merri had to strain her eyeballs to see Brandon's response in her peripheral vision.

"She's not my girlfriend."

Please don't tell them I'm with the Colby Agency. Merri prayed he would keep that info to himself for the moment. They would know who she was from her ID in her purse. But there was a difference between being a friend or girlfriend than being an investigator on official business.

"If this is about my friend…my roommate," Brandon told the man, "I don't know anything about his work or his murder. I've already told the police that trying to get information from me is a waste of time. There's nothing to get."

Merri swung her gaze to the man poking her with the gun. "We're not the police, Thomas," the bastard warned, his lips twisting slightly with smugness. "We don't care what you've told anyone else. You will tell us what you know before you die." He shifted his attention to Merri. "That's a promise to both of you."

He drew the muzzle away from her and backed up a step. "You have one hour. Think long and hard about your answer before I come back. If you don't have what I'm looking for, then you'll both die."

When the door had closed behind the gunman, Merri turned to Brandon. "You okay?" She struggled to slow her breathing. Damn, that was close.

Brandon closed in on her. "Am I

okay?" He looked her over. "You're the one who had the gun in your face. Are *you* okay?"

"I'm okay." She dragged in another deep breath, told herself to remain calm. She'd been in similar circumstances before. It wasn't as if this was the first time she'd faced the threat of death.

"You were going to tell me something," he said, suspicion in those dark eyes again. "Something you said you should have told me already."

"First," she offered, she was rationalizing, using excuses to avoid the inevitable, "we have to find a way to get out of here."

He glanced around the room. No windows. One locked door. "You can't be serious."

Merri summoned the fire that she refused to let die. "You came to me for help. Trust me. We will get out of here before that bastard comes back."

She had no idea how, but somehow.

As for her deafness, no need to worry her client about that right now.

She could tell him later…when staying alive wasn't an issue.

Chapter Four

9:20 p.m.

She had to think.

Fifty-five minutes and they could very well be dead.

"These men…to kill us."

Merri stared up at Brandon. Struggled a moment to fill in the parts she had missed. Clearly he had never been in this situation before and he was scared. As he should be.

"Unless you give them what they want," she countered, an idea coming to her.

Her suggestion wasn't exactly a palatable option, but it might buy them a little much-needed time. Unless she came up with something better, that might very well be their only option.

He stared at her as if she'd lost her mind.

Maybe she had.

"Just let me do the talking," she said, in case anyone was listening. "Neither of us wants to die just because your roommate was into something he shouldn't have been." When he would have interrupted, she held up a hand to silence him. "These guys don't want us at all. They want the video Kick had. This isn't really about us. I know you want to clear yourself with the police, but this is about saving our lives. We can deal with the police later."

The confusion marring his brow told her that he didn't get it. Thankfully, however, he did as she'd asked and kept his mouth shut.

Heart thudding, Merri turned and

strode to the door. She had to do this right the first time. If she missed anything their captor said, she could screw this up. There wouldn't likely be any second chances. She tightened her fingers into a fist and pounded on the door.

She swallowed, prayed that whoever was on the other side of that steel door hadn't responded verbally to her banging. When five trauma-filled seconds had passed, she reached up to beat on the door once more. It swung inward, she scarcely backed up in time to prevent the damned thing from smacking her in the face.

"Eight minutes," proclaimed the same man who had pushed them into the room. "Didn't take too long to decide that staying alive was more appealing than being dead. Aren't we proud of ourselves?"

Oh, yes, proud beyond words. And he had been listening. "Look." Merri braced her hands on her hips and stood toe-to-

toe with the man. He was a good half foot taller than her and his age was showing. What she could see of his hair was gray, and he had a bit of a thick middle. No doubt the guy in charge at field level. "All we're trying to do is stay out of trouble," she allowed. "Brandon didn't kill his roommate. The guy was a total jerk but he didn't deserve to die." She shrugged. "As far as I'm concerned, he got what he deserved. I didn't know him that well. The only thing we're trying to do is stay out of trouble with the police. Problem is, we don't have a clue what Kick was up to, but we do have some idea of where he may have hidden what you're looking for."

The corners of those watchful eyes crinkled as he narrowed them in suspicion. "If you don't know what he was up to, why would you think you know where he'd hidden what we're looking for?"

Fair question. "Because he told us he

was in trouble." That was the truth as far as Merri knew. "He gave Brandon a package in case something happened to him." Since she'd made up that part of the story, she glanced briefly at her client to judge his reaction to where she was going. His brown eyes were wide with worry. "We can take you to the package. My guess is that's what you're looking for."

"How 'bout you give me the location and I'll check it out. If the package contains what we're looking for, I'll tell my men to let you go."

Though she couldn't hear the nuances of his tone, she didn't miss the haughty expression, the certainty in his eyes. He wanted the information, then he wanted both her and Brandon out of the way. There would be no letting them go.

"We could," she offered, "but that scenario wouldn't be in our best interests. Neither of us presents a threat to you. We take you to the package, you get what you want and we get our freedom. Seems like the perfect compromise to me."

He studied her eyes a moment. Assessing. "I checked out your ID, Ms. Walters. You work for a private investigations agency."

She lifted her chin in defiance of the fear that niggled at her determination. "That's right. I'm a researcher. That's why Brandon thought of me when he followed Kick's bizarre order."

The gray-haired man looked from Merri to Brandon and back. "How do I know you're not an investigator? Maybe he—" he hitched his thumb toward Brandon "—hired you to find the video for his own purposes."

She didn't have to ask for a clarification of what he meant by that last statement. Clearly the video contained some sort of evidence valuable enough to merit a blackmail situation for someone prestigious enough to be nervous. She laughed. "Do I look like an investigator to you?" At a couple inches over five feet and a lean one hundred pounds, she didn't exactly possess the stature to physically intimidate.

"I run background searches all day," she went on. "I dig up info. That's it. Brandon is my boyfriend. He didn't tell you that because he was afraid you'd do just what you did—try hurting me to get him to cooperate. I'm trying to help him. The only reason he didn't tell the police about the package was because I was afraid of him doing anything until we figured out if doing so was in his best interests."

Brandon was suddenly at her side. "…person I can trust to help me with this. We can give you what you want. We don't care about whatever Kick was working on. We just want to be left alone."

Merri caught the latter part of his disclaimer before swinging her attention back to the man standing between them and freedom.

"Tell me where the package is—" the

man withdrew his weapon "—or I'll finish this now."

The business end of the gun bored into Merri's chest. Her heart bumped her sternum in protest. He was doing it again. Jerk.

Brandon started to push between her and the weapon. He said something but Merri didn't get it. What she did get was that he shouldn't take risks like that when a weapon was drawn and leveled.

"Back off, lover boy," the man warned.

Merri placed a hand on Brandon's arm. His gaze swung to her. She shook her head at him, then promptly returned her attention to the man with the gun.

"Give me the location."

Fine. "At my agency." She held her breath. Brandon stared at her as if she'd lost her mind—again.

The tension ramped higher as the bastard stared at her. Then his lips moved. "You can't be serious."

It was the perfect setup for her and

Brandon. But it sucked big-time for the man with the weapon in his hand. "I locked the package in my desk. I knew it would be safe there." Damn straight. The only thing locked in her desk that was important to her at the moment was her weapon. Not to mention, she'd just given this dirtbag a no-win situation. Now the ball was in his court.

"I'll need the key." He thrust out his free hand.

She moved her head side to side and heaved a heavy breath. "I'm afraid it's not that simple. The building is locked down for the weekend. Security is the best available. On-site personnel as well as high-tech surveillance. You won't get in after business hours without risking alerting security and the authorities." The Colby Agency had survived that kind of intrusion. Anyone getting in after lockdown would have had to do some major planning or gotten lucky about rounds the way Brandon had. Even the best security personnel went a little lax on a holiday weekend.

There were more of those pulse-pounding moments of no reaction.

Finally the man with the gun made his decision. "No problem. We'll take the two of you there. You go in and get the package. The cops show up or you don't come back, your boyfriend dies. You come back without what we want, you both die."

Simple enough.

10:55 p.m.

"REMEMBER."

Merri focused hard on the man's lips. He'd turned to stare at her from the front seat. The dim light of the van's dash was all that allowed her to see the movement as he spoke. She couldn't afford to miss a word, though she felt confident she knew what he had to say.

"You go in, get the package and come straight back to the van." He hitched his head toward where Brandon sat in the back, an accomplice holding a gun to his head. "You don't come back, you call the police, you make a single move we don't like and he dies."

"I understand." Merri reached for the handle of the sliding door. She didn't dare turn her back until she was absolutely certain the man in charge had nothing else to say. "Anything else?"

He shoved her purse at her. "Go." His lips tightened into a firm line, indicating his lack of patience and no small amount of fury.

Merri hung the bag's strap on her shoulder, opened the sliding door and hopped out. She sent Brandon one last reassuring look, hoped he understood that she would figure something out. Then she turned and walked steadily toward the building's front entrance. Her mind spun with a multitude of scenarios. It didn't matter if she produced what the man wanted; he intended to kill both her and Brandon.

She had to come up with a plan.

At the door, she reached into her purse and dug for her badge. Her cell was missing, of course—she'd seen it on the dash of the van. The bastard had obviously picked it up back in the alley. Pepper spray was missing, too. She slid the badge through the reader and the lock mechanism released immediately.

With a deep breath she opened the door and stepped into the lobby. The security guard, Raymond Shooke, was watching her from his position behind the reception desk. He smiled and said, "What brings you back here this late the night before Christmas Eve, Ms. Walters?"

She manufactured a smile. "Left something in my office. I won't be long."

Raymond moved his head side to side. "Bless your heart. You've had a busy night. Least you won't be alone."

Merri hesitated. She had to be careful here. The man in the van would be watching her with binoculars. The massive glass front allowed a clear view into the lobby. No missteps.

"Someone else from the Colby Agency is here?"

Raymond nodded. "Simon Ruhl."

Why would he be here? Before she could voice the question, the guard went on, "I'm sorry, Ms. Walters. I know it's none of my business but when you left with that gentleman…" He shrugged. "I was worried. Since I wasn't at the desk when that gentleman came in and he looked a little strange, I felt I should let Mr. Ruhl know what had gone down on my watch."

Equal measures of relief and fear rushed through Merri's veins. "I'm sorry I worried you, Raymond. The gentleman I left with is a new client. He really is okay, as I told you." She'd assured the guard when she left with Brandon to go to his apartment that all was well. Evidently because she was Merrilee Walters, the new deaf investigator, he'd felt compelled to call in any suspicious activity.

That's unfair, Merri. Simon probably instructed security to watch out for her. Not Raymond's fault.

Raymond smiled. "The nature of the business draws some strange folks, ma'am. It's my job to double-check anything I feel uncertain about."

"Of course." She gestured toward the bank of elevators. "I'll just go up and explain things to Simon."

Raymond nodded. "Yes, ma'am."

Merri headed for the elevators, her pulse rate racing. Simon had likely attempted to call her cell. She hadn't thought to check it while she was at Brandon's apartment. Then the bad guys had shown up and everything had gone crazy.

Simon would not be happy. It was a miracle he hadn't already called in backup from Ian and/or some of the others. It wouldn't be pretty.

Problem was, she had no idea how she was going to explain this to him and have him understand.

Brandon's life depended on the next few minutes, which would play out based on her every move.

No pressure there.

She rode to the agency's floor and stepped into the reception lobby. No sign of Simon. With a deep breath, she headed for his office. They ran into each other as she turned into the door.

Before he spoke, he looked her up and down. "You okay? I've been trying to reach you on your cell for the last hour. Ian is on his way."

Damn it. That was what she hadn't wanted to happen. "Get him on the phone now," Merri urged. Simon's gaze narrowed. Before he could voice his concern, she said, "Hurry. Tell him to park near the rear exit. He cannot come into the front parking area or the building's lower level garage. Brandon will die if he does."

Simon pulled out his phone and entered Ian's speed dial number. Thankfully, he didn't ask any questions. Merri watched his lips closely as he related her instructions to Ian. Then he added, "I don't know what's going on, but I'll call you back in a few minutes with an update." He closed the phone and slid it back into his jacket pocket. "All right, what's going on?"

She gave him a condensed version. She didn't have time to spell out every detail. "Two men are in that van in the front lot. One has a gun to Brandon's head. They're going to kill him." Either way, she didn't have to add. Simon knew moreso than she what was on the agenda of the men holding Brandon hostage.

Simon hesitated only a moment. "Let's give him what he wants."

Relief flooded Merri. "We need a

video storage device. One that isn't common."

Simon grabbed her by the elbow and rushed toward the research department. Every imaginable storage device could be found in the supply closet there.

Once in the massive room with its half a dozen desks, Simon turned to her. "Get a padded envelope and put your client's name on it."

Merri rushed to the drawers of the common storage cabinet near the shared printer, found what she needed and went to a desk to get a marker for labeling the envelope. She called to mind what Kick's handwriting looked like and wrote Brandon Thomas on the envelope.

Simon had moved to a computer at one of the desks. She moved up behind him and watched as he downloaded a video from a research file that included some covert surveillance of a former client. He cut the file before the face of the man being monitored came into view. A full three minutes of footage. He removed the device and passed it to her. She placed it in the envelope and sealed the flap.

"You know you can't go back out there," Simon said when her gaze landed on his face once more.

She nodded. That would be a death sentence for both her and Brandon.

"He has your cell phone?"

She nodded. "It's on the dash of the van." She'd noticed it there as she'd gotten out.

"Good." Simon stood. "Let's go to your office."

Merri had an idea where this was going. She just hoped it would work. When they reached her office, Simon indicated the phone on her desk, the one designed for the hearing impaired. "Call your cell and tell your captor that you'll meet him at the front entrance. You'll trade the package for Brandon, then he can drive away."

"He warned that if I made one misstep he would kill Brandon."

Simon's gaze locked with hers. "He'll kill both of you if you go back out there."

No question. "So I tell him to come to the door with Brandon. I give him the package. He lets Brandon come inside. The door locks. The glass is bulletproof."

"I'll contact the police and have them head this way so they can surround the van in the parking lot before the bastards get away. It only takes a couple of minutes. I know the captain of one of the teams who specialize in just this sort of situation. I'll tell him not to move in until I give the word. I'll monitor the situation from Victoria's office. When you give Raymond the word, he'll buzz Victoria's office and I'll tell the team to move in."

Victoria Colby-Camp's office over-looked the street as well as the small visitor parking area in front. As the head of the Colby Agency, there was an alarm wired directly from the security desk to her office.

"I'll let Raymond know what's going on. He can appear to step away from his desk and monitor you and the entrance from nearby."

Merri kept picturing Brandon's face. He was depending solely on her to make sure he got out of this alive. But Simon was right. This was their best shot at survival. "Okay."

As Simon stepped out of her office to put through his call, Merri made *the* call. She had to call twice before the bastard answered her phone. Though her cell was equipped for the hearing impaired, it operated as a regular cell phone unless that particular software was enabled with the push of a button on the side of the phone.

"You're running out of time," the man said. Merri read his words on the screen on her desk phone.

"I have the package," she said flatly.

"If you want it, bring Brandon to the front entrance and I'll exchange the package for him."

Silence. When no words appeared on the screen her heart surged into her throat. She wasn't sure her phone could relay the sound of a gunshot in words.

"No way. Get down here now or he dies."

Merri bit her lip. What if this was a mistake? What if Simon was wrong? What if... This was the only option. "Look," she said, "I really like my boyfriend, but I'm not ready to die for him. If I come out there, you'll kill us both. I don't care about you or whoever is paying you or anything else. Just bring him to the door and we'll exchange. You drive away with what you came for and we get to stay alive. It's very simple."

"Just so you know," he boasted, "I'm monitoring the police bands as we speak. If you've called the police, your boyfriend will pay the price."

Fear pounded in her brain. "You said I shouldn't call the police," she said, hopefully loud enough for Simon to hear. "Why would I do that? I don't care about that. I only care about keeping myself and my boyfriend alive through this."

Simon came into the room as she spoke. He stepped around her desk and viewed the screen. He shook his head and gave her that look that said she had nothing to worry about on that score.

More breath-stealing silence elapsed.

"Okay. I will meet you at the door for the exchange. But just because you don't see a gun doesn't mean one isn't zeroed in right on your pretty head. So watch your step."

"I understand."

The line went dead.

Merri placed the handset back in the cradle. She turned to Simon. "Your captain friend is bringing in his team dark?"

"Absolutely. And Ian is waiting in his

car west of the rear entrance. Whatever we need him to do, he's prepared to act."

"I don't know who is behind this threat," Merri explained. "But I'm not sure it will be over just because we take down these guys. Unless they talk, it's doubtful that we'll get to the bottom of Brandon's problem." Not to mention that the police consider him a suspect—the *only* suspect—in Kick Randolph's murder.

"We'll deal with that when the time comes," her superior assured her. "For now, stick with the plan and whatever happens do *not* step outside the door. Stay behind the bulletproof glass."

Enough said. Simon's instincts were right on target. She hadn't expected any less from this experienced man. She had to trust that he knew what he was doing.

"Okay." Merri's fingers tightened on the package. "Let's do this, then."

The ride down in the elevator seemed to vanquish the last of the air in her lungs. Simon had moved to Victoria's office to monitor the situation in the parking lot from her massive window. Ian waited in the rear as requested.

There was every reason to believe that this would end well for all involved, except the bad guys.

But there was so much she still didn't know…that Brandon didn't know.

That he might not live to know.

Merri understood his special circumstances; she wanted to help him. If what she suspected was true, he might end up behind bars for a crime he hadn't committed.

He needed her help.

But they had to survive this night first.

Raymond had already left his post as per Simon's instructions by the time she arrived in the lobby. Exactly as planned.

Think positively, Merri.

This had to work.

Simon knew what he was doing even if she hesitated or had a misstep. He would have a Plan B.

At the door, she peered through the protective glass at the nondescript white van that waited in the lot.

Stay calm. Do what you have to do. Show this guy that sheer desperation and determination are your motives. Not that the police was standing by or that Ian and Simon were now on the case.

She waved the envelope. Waited. Nothing or no one moved. She waved it again. "Come on. I'm not coming to you."

Please, God, don't let Brandon get killed.

The front passenger door as well as the sliding door behind it opened simultaneously.

Merri held her breath.

The man who appeared to be in charge of this operation left his door open and stepped toward the opening where Brandon waited. He grabbed Brandon by the arm and started toward the building, hauling his captive at his side.

The streetlights beamed their glow

across the dark lot. No other vehicles waited. Nothing moved except the man with the gun.

And Brandon.

As they neared the building, Merri fortified her defenses. She was unarmed, but that was necessary. She resurrected the proper emotions for him to see.

The two men stopped in front of the door. Merri pushed the inside release with her free hand and held the door open just far enough for Brandon to come inside.

"Send him inside and I'll toss you the envelope." She stared directly at the man in charge. His partner no doubt had a bead on her or Brandon from his position inside the dark interior of the van.

"No way. Toss me the envelope, let me confirm that it contains what I need and then I'll release him."

Thankfully Brandon continued to keep quiet. He couldn't possibly have any idea that help was all around them. Merri would have to show her appreciation for his trust later.

She tossed the envelope to the man. Simon had told her not to step outside the door. She wasn't about to disobey his order.

The man passed the envelope to Brandon. "Open it."

Hands shaking, Brandon picked at the tab until it slid across the length of the envelope. He passed it back to the man next to him.

The bastard pulled the compact storage device from inside. He frowned, then looked at Merri. "If what we're looking for is not on here, we'll be back." His gaze narrowed. "Trust me. There won't be any place you can hide from us." He glanced at Brandon, then turned his attention back to Merri. "No place on Earth. You understand me?"

She nodded, amping up the fear on her face.

He pushed Brandon toward her and

turned to hustle back to the van. Merri got a glimpse of the man inside, his weapon trained on her even as the jerk walked away. She yanked Brandon inside, then pulled the door closed.

Relief flooded her, making her legs weak.

"What…the hell did…give him?"

"Let's go." She didn't have time to ask him to repeat what he'd said. Instead, she started backing across the lobby, Brandon in tow. Before they reached the halfway mark, two dark vans barreled into the small lot and SWAT personnel spilled from the open doors.

A satisfied smile tickled her lips. "That's how the game is played," she muttered to herself. Chalk one up for the Colby Agency.

A burst of light and flame split the darkness.

The floor shook beneath her feet.

The official personnel in black charging

forward were tossed about and thrown to the ground.

Merri stared in disbelief at what was left of the white van. Mangled metal and fierce flames shooting toward the night sky were all that remained.

The van had exploded with the two would-be killers inside.

How was that possible? Would the two men have pushed some sort of self-destruct button just to protect the person in charge?

That didn't seem possible. Yet it had happened.

And she still had no proof that Brandon was innocent. Their one lead had just gone up in flames.

Chapter Five

Christmas Eve, 2:15 a.m.

Brandon felt as if he were sitting in a corner after being caught cutting class. The investigator who'd willingly took his case, Merri Walters, and her associates were squaring off in the conference room of the Colby Agency.

The one named Simon Ruhl agreed with Merri's conclusion that whoever had sent those men, possibly some of the ones Brandon and Merri had glimpsed at the warehouse, were more than prepared to finish the job. The authorities had confirmed that two bodies were discovered amid the remains of the van.

Brandon swallowed back the lump of anxiety clogging his throat. He would be dead right now if not for Merri's quick thinking.

She had saved his life. The risk she had chosen to take was the only one that would have worked. Period. It had been a shot in the dark but the only one they'd had. Her associate, Ruhl, had played his hand with the SWAT folks perfectly. Yet the end result had backfired.

Brandon had to come clean with Merri soon. She'd risked a hell of a lot to help him and the job wasn't finished yet. He owed her an explanation. He'd watched how she analyzed him. How she rephrased questions to help him respond rationally. She suspected there was a problem in how he processed information.

She deserved the whole truth.

"This is a mistake," Ian Michaels announced. He was totally against Merri continuing to handle Brandon's case alone. The aloof man had scarcely spared Brandon a glance. Not that Brandon could blame him. Not really. He'd rushed into the agency's offices without checking in with security. Then he'd been the cause of one investigator being abducted along with him. And if that wasn't enough, he'd generated havoc in the agency's parking lot. Two more people were dead. Good or bad, dead was dead.

Talk about getting off on the wrong foot.

"We have the clues," Merri argued. "All we have to do at this point is see where they lead us. We have to know what we're up against before taking measures to protect our client."

"Not exactly a stellar starting place," Michaels argued. "Our *client* is a homicide suspect with killers right on his heels. In case you haven't noticed, we're dealing with professionals here. Not some fired-up bad guys who want to interfere with whatever this Randolph fellow was up to. This is no mere grudge, Ms. Walters. This is serious. Very serious.

"As we've deducted," he continued before Merri could react verbally, "there will be more. Friends or associates of the dead men, perhaps. Whoever comes after Mr. Thomas next time won't take any chances. They will learn from this mistake and shoot first, then ask questions later."

"I would agree with you," Merri countered quickly, "but if the goal is to gain access to the evidence, taking us alive will be the ultimate objective in any scenario. Don't you agree?"

"I agree," Ruhl offered, his posture and tone far more amiable than his colleague's. "Our only option, as I see it, is that you and Mr. Thomas plunge into your search for the video and/or written evidence while we run interference from this end. The police will be all over this."

Michaels pushed out of his chair and walked to the window. He thrust his hands into his pockets and leaned a hip on the window ledge.

Brandon couldn't help holding his breath. Though Mr. Ruhl appeared to want to allow Merri to help Brandon, Michaels seemed to be the one with the power to make the ultimate decision. Not good for Brandon.

"That could work," Michaels agreed, "except we have no evidence of who these men were. We don't know who hired them. We don't even know what they're after." He sent a pointed look at Brandon. "We don't actually know anything except that three men are dead."

"Finding the answers to those questions," Merri insisted, drawing her superior's intense scrutiny once more, "is the only way to clear Brandon of the murder as well as keep him alive."

"You're certain that's what you want to do?" Michaels asked Merri, his tone less stern. His expression was almost compassionate. "Despite the stumbling block that could prove detrimental to your survival as well as his?"

They stared at each other for a full ten seconds. "Yes." Merri stood her ground. "I am fully capable of conducting this investigation."

Brandon couldn't help wondering if that last exchange had been about him and his personal *situation.* It sure as hell sounded as if that was the case.

"Well, then," Michaels pushed off the ledge, looked directly at Merri, "I suppose you should get started. I'm certain whoever hired those men is fully aware what has occurred and likely has this building under surveillance as we speak."

Brandon blocked the worry that accompanied those very true words. Maybe he should just try to find Kick's stuff alone. This nightmare had put Merri in serious danger already. He shouldn't be dragging anyone else into this, not after all that had happened. His mind kept playing the apartment and van explosions over and over in his head.

But could he do this alone?

The answer was easy—no. Obviously Merri had already warned her associates as to the severity of Brandon's personal challenge. That pointed exchange between her and Michaels left no question. She'd figured it out on her own. Brandon should have just told her from the start. But he hadn't.

He'd learned the hard way that discovering his challenge changed people's perspective about him. They saw nothing else after that. He already had enough black marks against him, considering he was the only suspect in his roommate's murder and he had no real idea what this whole thing was really about. Anything more, and he was sure Merri wouldn't want his case at all. It was a miracle that she did at this point.

"First," Ruhl suggested, "we have to

get the two of you out the door under the radar of anyone who might be watching."

Despite the decision to take his case, the two men continued to speak directly to Merri. Brandon supposed he should be thankful he wasn't on his own with this. He wasn't sure what he would have done if he'd been forced to walk out the door with no support from the Colby Agency. He could deal with them acting as if he weren't in the room and speaking directly to Merri.

The agency's reputation was what had brought him here. He'd heard Kick talk about the best private investigators in the nation and the Colby Agency had ranked right up there at the top. Chances were he would never have remembered the remark, except that when he left the precinct after being interrogated for hours he'd noticed a business card on the ground while waiting at the bus stop.

The Most Private Of Investigations: The Colby Agency.

Brandon had known what he had to do.

"Let's go," Merri said to him.

He hadn't realized she had walked up to where he sat. He blinked, pushed to his feet. "What happens now?" He'd heard the decision, but he couldn't recall the sequence of events as outlined by Mr. Ruhl.

"Two more cars are on the way to the rear entrance. Slade Convoy and Ted Tallant will pull up behind Ian's car at the rear entrance. You'll exchange coats with Ian, then you, Ian and I will load into the three different vehicles, taking different directions. We'll rendezvous when it's safe to do so."

Brandon hesitated, giving Michaels and Ruhl time to leave the room since they were on their way out anyway. He searched Merri's face then. "Are you sure you want to do this?" There was something about her…the way she ignored him when she chose. As if she hadn't heard whatever he'd said or noticed something that had happened. But then, he had been in a full-blown panic most of the evening. It was possible that he was reading between lines that weren't there.

Merri placed a hand on his arm. She'd done that a couple of times tonight. Brandon couldn't remember when a mere touch had given him so much confidence. It was as if she understood him thoroughly—which wasn't possible. She didn't know the truth, didn't know his awful secret. With each passing moment, sharing that awful part of who he was became more difficult.

"Don't worry," she assured him when he definitely didn't deserve her assurance, "we'll figure this out. The Colby Agency is the best. We'll find the truth and see that the person responsible for Kick's murder pays."

Fear nagged at Brandon. When she discovered a certain truth about him, would she still want to be a part of this?

He nodded. "All right."

She flashed him one last smile and headed for the door.

Why the hell didn't he just tell her?

"Merri!"

She kept walking, disappearing into the corridor.

He shook his head and went after her. Maybe the fact that she hadn't heard him was a sign for him to keep his mouth shut for now. Too bad he didn't believe in those kinds of signs.

Images from his apartment…finding his roommate dead on the floor…all the blood. He'd tried to help Kick but it had been too late. Then the explosion. Two explosions, no less.

He was friendless…homeless.

Damn. His feet slowed, allowing Merri to get even farther ahead of him. Kick was dead. And he had no place to go when this was over.

Assuming he was still alive when it was over.

MERRI CHECKED HER PURSE once more to see that she'd gotten everything she needed. Cell phone—she kept a backup in her desk. Weapon. Her fingers glided over the smooth steel. She'd thought those days were over. The Colby Agency had an outstanding record when it came to solving cases without excessive force. Just her luck to get the case that was the exception. She had cash. And a few other toys Simon had ensured she took with her. GPS, couple of communication devices, and two tracking devices— all miniscule in size. Except for the GPS, it was about the size of her cell phone.

She was good to go.

Simon tapped her on the arm. She met

his expectant gaze. "Ian finally lost his tail," he explained.

"Excellent."

Ian had insisted on being Brandon's driver. Ted Tallant had ridden with him in case he needed backup in the way of firepower. Slade Convoy had driven his own vehicle.

Apparently whoever had been watching the agency had decided that Ian was Brandon, since he'd been wearing Brandon's coat and he had dark hair, a little long like the other man's. Ted had used Merri's coat to cover his head and the upper part of his body. Since the guy was seriously taller than Merri, she was surprised those conducting the surveillance had been fooled. Then again, Brandon was the target. More likely they had decided to follow him whether Merri was with him or not.

The three vehicles would rendezvous at Lincoln Park. Merri and Brandon would take Simon's car and go to the Colby safe house.

Off the beaten path and near the water, the place was a palace. Built when Victoria's son was a child, the house had stood empty for many, many years. It was only the last few years that Victoria and her family had started to use it again for weekend getaways. There were a lot of bad memories there. Jim, Victoria's son, had gone missing from that yard.

Just went to show that beauty and elegance couldn't protect a person when evil lurked nearby.

The house was a state-of-the-art fortress now. Merri and Brandon would be safe there, for sure. The time and space they needed for getting to the bottom of this puzzle would be available. Bridget Turner, a research analyst at the agency, had been assigned to work on putting the few lines together or sorting out possible meanings. Merri didn't hold out much hope for any real results. She was certain the answers lay one place only—Brandon Thomas's head. She had to find a way to draw out the meanings behind those phrases. Randolph wouldn't have used those phrases if they hadn't meant something to Brandon.

All she had to do was figure out how those pieces fit into the puzzle of his life.

That thought dragged her back to the idea that something wasn't quite right with Brandon. She had her suspicions but she couldn't be sure. Not one hundred percent. Pushing him for an answer would only make him question her. He'd noticed something was off with her, but the situation hadn't allowed for follow-up.

It was coming.

She understood that with complete certainty.

Simon braked to a stop along the sidewalk on a deserted stretch of street. Ian's sedan was already parked up the block. Slade's sedan eased to a stop some thirty or so feet behind Simon's.

Simon turned to Merri. "Do not hesitate to call upon me if you need anything at all. Research will be in touch regarding what they turn up."

Merri nodded. "Thank you for backing me up."

The man she felt closer to than anyone else at the agency smiled. "Don't make me regret it."

With that he emerged from the car and walked toward where Ian had parked. Merri got out and went around to the driver's side. She didn't miss the look Ian sent her way. The streetlight didn't allow her to overlook the worry on his face. He didn't like this one bit.

Wearing his own coat once more, Brandon joined her. "Can you tell me where we're going? Mr. Michaels didn't have much to say on the way here."

Merri nodded to the car. "Let's get going. I'll explain on the way."

As she drove away from the rendezvous point, she didn't look back. She didn't need to. Ian and Simon would still be debating this decision. She had to do this right so Ian would at last fully trust her. More important, she couldn't let Simon down.

Any more than she could Brandon.

Merri tried her best to fill every second of the trip with dialogue. If she gave Brandon an opportunity to speak he would notice that she didn't hear him. Only when she stopped at an intersection did she pause and look his way, inviting his comments.

"I suppose you're right," he allowed, "Michaels was a little busy evading that tail. It probably wasn't personal."

"Exactly." When she'd run out of anything else to tell him about the safe house, she'd explained that Ian likely hadn't been slighting him en route, but had focused on the task at hand.

"Here we are," she announced as she made the final turn to the safe house address. She'd only been here once. She entered the code for the gate, then glanced at her passenger as the gates slid open.

"Wow…"

"I had the same reaction the first time I came here." Though she didn't catch all that he'd said, judging by what she could see of his expression, he was impressed. She had already explained about Victoria's family, including the harrowing years her son was missing.

"Housekeeping came while we were en route and stocked the kitchen and anything else we might need. Like clothes and toiletries." She was thankful for that since she could definitely use a shower and clean clothes.

As she rounded the hood to meet Brandon in front of the parked car, he said, "The Colby Agency thinks of everything."

"We try."

At the front entrance she entered the security code that she had memorized, then pressed her thumb to the scanner for final identification. No key was required. Only the code and an authenticated fingerprint. Simple, yet nearly impossible to breach.

Inside she closed the door and reset the alarm. She turned in time to see Brandon's lips moving. "…Colby must be rich."

"Victoria has worked a lot of years to reach this point of financial comfort." Merri had a great deal of respect for the woman. She hadn't been born into this level of wealth. She and both her husbands had worked hard to reach this pinnacle. "Come on, I'll show you to your room."

The house had a number of bedrooms. Clients were usually housed in the far room upstairs, leaving the others—closer to the staircase—for their protectors, in this case for Merri.

The light was on in the last bedroom down the long hall on the second floor. Two changes of clothes, in addition to toiletries and sleepwear, were carefully laid out on the bed.

Merri didn't have to look to know that the clothes would be the correct size. She'd estimated Brandon's sizes and passed them along to Simon.

Brandon was talking again, his attention still focused on the items spread across the luxurious bed.

"What?" She stepped closer, waiting for him to turn his face toward her.

He shrugged. "I was just saying that this is incredible." He searched her eyes. "You know, I didn't even ask." His mouth worked a moment before readable words were formed. "I'm not sure I can afford your fee. I should have asked before—" he gestured to the room at large "—all this." His arms dropped to his sides. "Before you risked your life." The regret in his expression dug at her heart.

"We take a few pro bono cases." She didn't want to make him feel bad about his inability to pay. "Sometimes," she went on, "justice doesn't have a price. We do what needs to be done."

He thought about that for a moment. Those dark eyes remained filled with uncertainty even as he spoke. "So what do we do now?"

Truth was, they had had quite a night. "We get some sleep." Personally, she was going to take a long hot bath and then sleep like the dead for at least a few hours. At his crestfallen expression, she added, "Then we'll dig in and figure out where those phrases lead us."

When she was about to turn away, he stopped her. "How is it that no one knows about this place?"

Translation: are you sure we're safe here?

"Victoria built this house a very long time ago, more than two decades ago. She didn't use it for a very long time. Most of her friends and associates believe she sold it. You have nothing to worry about here." She lifted her shoulders, then let them fall. "There's nothing to be afraid of, you have my word. Even if somehow those yahoos followed us, there's an alarm system that is what all other state-of-the-art systems aspire to be. We're hooked directly into the agency. And—" she patted her purse "—I'm armed."

He stared at her purse a moment. "Do you know how to use it?"

One corner of her mouth lifted in a knowing half smile. God, she was tired. "I definitely know how to use it. I worked as a homicide detective in Nashville for several years before coming to the Colby Agency."

"Was there trouble in your past career?" He watched her closely in an attempt to read what her words wouldn't tell him. "Is that why you moved here? Or why Mr. Michaels sounded as if he would prefer some other investigator work my case?"

Ah, so he'd noticed Ian's innuendo in the conference room. "No. No trouble. I just decided I wanted to do something different. And Ian didn't want me to take your case because I'm fairly new at the agency. He would have preferred a more experienced investigator." That was true, in part.

Brandon's brow furrowed. "If you used to be a homicide detective in your former job, it makes sense to me that Michaels would consider you the best person for the job."

Good point. She wasn't going there. "Get some sleep, Brandon. You're going to need it just as much as I do. We'll talk about the case later when we're rested and our heads are clear."

She exited the room before he could ask another question. A long hot bath was on her agenda. In her room, the one next to Brandon's, there was a comfy night-gown and two changes of clothes. Not colors she would have picked—she liked bright colors—but she could live with it. The selections had been made with blending in mind. Beiges, tans and browns.

The bed looked so inviting, she scarcely worked up the wherewithal to go for that bath.

But her aching muscles would thank her when she awakened a few hours from now.

She turned on the faucet in the big, jetted tub, and adjusted the temperature of the water. She stripped off her clothes and stepped into the ankle-deep water. Waiting until it had filled was out of the question. A variety of bath salts and bubbly, scented oil lined the tiled edge. She picked one, poured it into the water and watched the scented bubbles build. Smelled good.

The water had reached her torso and she leaned back, letting her skin adjust to the cool feel of the tub, and closed her eyes. That wouldn't last long. Soon the water and the tub would be nice and hot all around her.

The bubbles tickled her breasts as the water level rose.

Heaven.

Her mind drifted, then floated away. God, she'd needed this.

Cool fingers touched her shoulder.

Her lids fluttered open and she sat up, crossing her arms over her breasts.

Brandon Thomas stood next to the tub, his eyes wide with something like frustration. But it was his bare chest that captured the better part of her attention. Wide shoulders, lean waist and lots of muscled terrain in between. The jeans hung low on his hips, giving just a glimpse of the dark, silky hair that veered down to off-limits territory.

"Is something wrong?" She really didn't know what else to say.

"The house phone is ringing off the hook." He planted his long-fingered hands on those lean hips. "Didn't you hear it?"

Of course she didn't. She was deaf.

But he didn't know that. She twisted the faucet knobs to the Off position then flashed him a proper glare. "I guess not." Her chin shot up a little higher as defiance arrowed through her. "The water was running and the door was closed." She wasn't sure about that last part, but maybe she'd closed it.

"What do you want me to do?"

Climb in here with me, she thought with a start. She blinked the idea away. She was tired. Not thinking straight. "I'll check the voice mail. If it's urgent," she said, nodding to her cell on the closed toilet lid, "whoever is calling will use my cell."

"Okay." He shrugged those incredibly wide shoulders. "Sorry." He glanced at the bubbles shielding her naked body. "I guess I'll go back to my room."

"I'll let you know if the call was news."

His dark, dark eyes meshed with hers and what she saw startled her all over again.

Approval. He liked what he saw.

She was the one wowed now.

But this was definitely not the time, much less the place.

He stalled at the door, turned back to her. The idea that her pulse rate had climbed significantly annoyed the heck out of her.

"It's Christmas Eve, you know."

"Yeah." A slight nod accompanied her response. She hadn't forgotten, but it was just another day to her this year. "Is that a problem for you?"

He gave that good-looking head a shake. Something else she shouldn't have noticed.

Depending upon how long it took them to figure this out, maybe she would take a break and look around for an artificial tree and decorations. There were lots of places around here to store stuff.

"Good night," she offered.

"'Night."

The door closed behind him.

Merri leaned back, tried to relax again. Maybe she was in over her head.

She hadn't heard the house phone and she damn sure hadn't heard him come into the room.

First thing after they'd had breakfast, she would tell him the truth.

It wasn't as if he could decide he wanted another investigator at this point.

She chewed her lower lip.

Could he?

Chapter Six

Christmas Eve, 1:52 p.m.

On the range. Nothing can change. My space and no place. Invisible.

Merri stared at the phrases she'd written on her notepad. She pursed her lips and took a moment to consider her thoughts before she spoke. "This has to mean the place where he grew up." They had gone over every other possibility. There were no other reasonable alternatives.

"Seems logical."

Brandon's noncommittal attitude was beginning to get on her nerves. They had awoken about ten. She'd prepared breakfast with his help. He'd wanted to know what the call was about last night. She hadn't mentioned it until he'd asked because the call was nothing important, just property security wanting to ensure that all was as it should be as they settled in for the remainder of the night. Routine call.

The staff at the agency knew to call her on her cell phone. The specially designed phone would blink, allowing her to see that a call was coming in.

For more than two hours after dragging themselves out of bed and having breakfast, they had been brainstorming the phrases Kick had given Brandon a while back. He couldn't recall exactly when he'd been given this information. Sometime during the past month. For a man barely thirty, he had a heck of a time remembering the little things. But then, she suspected there was a reason for that. One he didn't want to talk about any more than she wanted to discuss being deaf.

Turner from Research had called. She'd come up with nothing more than what they had surmised on their own. Kick's selection of phrases wasn't related to any former headline or book or even a movie—at least not according to the elaborate software system employed by the Colby computers.

Kick had apparently been very careful not to connect his message to anything that would allow for easy access or misinterpretation. In doing so, he'd left Merri, who knew nothing about him other than what Google and Brandon had told her, to attempt to piece together a revealing message with little or no foundation in reasoning or logic.

"Where did Kick grow up?" she asked.

Brandon dropped back onto the sofa. Like Merri, he was still exhausted. "Blue Island. Maybe forty-five minutes from our old apartment."

The deceased's childhood home remained the only reasonable conclusion. "Home doesn't usually change." Unless there's a death or a divorce. "Home would certainly be his space and yet no place. Particularly if he didn't have any fond memories of growing up or if he hadn't been able to wait to get away."

Brandon sat up straight. "Wait. There was something he always said." His forehead furrowed in concentration. "That he was nobody growing up—invisible. He always dreamed of making it big in the city. That's why this story was so important to him. He wanted to prove they were wrong—the kids he grew up with, I mean."

"Invisible." That certainly covered the final part of the puzzle and fell in line with the rest of Merri's conclusions.

Brandon braced his forearms on his knees and searched Merri's eyes. A little shiver tangoed up her spine. *Stop,* she ordered. Not allowed. She'd spent way too much time in the past getting personally involved with one aspect or another of a case. Wasn't going to happen this time. The Colby Agency was a new beginning for her, professionally and personally.

"Since our apartment is history," Brandon continued, "and the bad guys no doubt still want to locate the video, we have to assume, I suppose, that they're probably watching any other place we might show up. They're expecting us to lead them to the evidence."

"Like the precinct where the investigation is assigned. The *Trib*. His girlfriend's place—if he had one." That was a question she should have already asked, but then the last twenty-four hours had been a little crazy. The last couple of hours had been the only time available for thinking.

"He didn't have a steady girlfriend," Brandon assured her. "Kick liked playing the field. No permanent attachments whatsoever, on or off the job. He liked his space."

"And the homes of any close family," Merri offered. "They'll be watching those, too."

"But we have to go to Blue Island."

She nodded. "We do." There was no better place to begin this search. "With the apartment gone and no girlfriend to check out, that leaves work and where he grew up."

Brandon's head was moving side to side before she finished her deductions. "No way would he leave anything important at the *Trib,* much less share even a hint of what he was working on with any of his colleagues. He claimed this was his big chance. He wasn't about to risk having anyone steal his glory."

"Blue Island it is, then." Merri reached for her phone to send Simon a text as to their plans. "I'll let the office know our strategy."

Brandon stood. She looked up at him.

"…to eat."

"Sure," she acknowledged though she hadn't gotten the entire sentence. She'd evolved into quite the expert at estimating what had likely been said. He was hungry. He wanted to eat. "I'll get something in a minute."

No sooner had she sent the text than the screen on her cell flashed, indicating that she had an incoming text.

Walters.

What's in Blue Island?

Simon.

We're relatively certain the puzzle or riddle or whatever the hell it is points to where he grew up. Kick, aka Kevin Randolph, grew up in Blue Island so that's where we'll go first.

Makes sense. Turner indicated his parents still live there and he has one sister, Bethany Stover, in the area, as well.

We'll be checking out both in addition to any neighbors or childhood friends we discover along the way.

Be careful, Merri.

Definitely.

A Detective Whitehall is in charge of the Randolph case. He's nosing around. I told him we're looking into the situation and that we'll keep him apprised.

Text his cell number to me and I'll touch base with him as soon as we determine if there's anything to know in Blue Island.

The Colby Agency had an outstanding reputation of cooperating with the local police. Keeping it that way was part of her job.

Is he aware that we're working with Brandon?

She typed the letters quickly across the screen.

In light of the two explosions, perhaps the police were having second thoughts about Brandon's suspected guilt.

Whitehall still considers Brandon a person of interest, but under the circumstances they're looking into his story about someone else being involved a bit more seriously.

At least the loss of Brandon's home was proving worthwhile on some level. Not to mention the two dead men in the mangled van. Simon reminded her once more to watch her back, then the exchange ended.

Merri had checked Randolph's two social network pages. Photos of his parents and sister were posted for public viewing. The men after Brandon would definitely be watching the homes of Randolph's immediate family. That meant going to those locations was risky business, but there was no way around it. Particular care would need to be taken on this field trip to Blue Island.

A hand waved in front of her face. She jumped, looked up to find Brandon hovering over her.

"You want a sandwich?"

She'd been so lost in thought she hadn't noticed that he'd walked back into the room. That had to stop. But there was only one way to do that. "Sure." She got to her feet and headed for the kitchen.

Brandon kept time with her pace. She glanced at him to see if he was speaking. He wasn't. Just watching her from the corners of his eyes.

She couldn't put off telling him the rest of the story much longer. Trust was key here, and she was showing a lack of it.

When they'd reached the island in the

massive kitchen, she saw that he'd spread all the sandwich fixings on the counter. She grabbed a couple of slices of bread. "Looks like there's a little of everything." Cheese, an array of sandwich meats, all the trimmings.

He picked up the thick sandwich he'd already prepared and tore off a bite. "Yep," he said between chews. "We wouldn't have to worry about going hungry any time soon around here."

Her gaze lingered on his lips when he licked them. She blinked, ordered herself to focus on preparing the sandwich. Focus on the case, Merri—not the man or his intensely dark eyes. With a soft drink from the fridge and her sandwich piled high, she headed back to the great room. She wanted to review her notes once more as she ate. And to avoid looking at him. Or his eyes.

Last night she hadn't really had much of a chance to analyze her new client. Now that she had the time, she recognized the too familiar mistake. On some level, whether her brain was ready to admit it or not, she was attracted to the guy. Maybe because he appeared to have a challenge of his own. The whole delay-confusion-memory sequence situation didn't sit right with her. Or maybe just because, to use a clichéd phrase, he was tall, dark and handsome.

Scanning her notes, she kept an eye on Brandon. He polished off his sandwich and went back for another. When the lunch clutter was cleaned up, they packed up their change of clothes and notes and headed for the car. So far, no more communication glitches.

She was thankful for the jeans, sweater and sneakers. Dressing up was something she did for work, but in her off time she lived in jeans. Hugging her parka a little closer as Brandon piled their stuff into the trunk, she worked at ignoring how his jeans molded to his backside. The size was a perfect fit. The shirt and sweater combination looked good on him. He'd been wearing sneakers already. She imagined that he lived in those just as she did when classier duds weren't required.

"Maybe I'll bring the laptop," she said when he turned around and caught her checking him out.

Before he could respond she dashed back to the house, provided the necessary security info and went inside. She slid the laptop into its case and grabbed the AC adapter and cord. When she returned to the door, she hesitated and watched Brandon. He surveyed the yard and the water beyond. Did he know more than he was telling her? She didn't think so. He was afraid of getting killed, but he was determined to do the right thing.

Going to the Randolph family would be tricky. Innocent or not, the police considered him a person of interest in the investigation—a suspect, really. The family would be aware of his standing with the police. Kick's parents might not want Brandon coming around, even if they could get close to the parents without getting caught by the enemy.

BRANDON VOLUNTEERED to drive. Mostly he wanted to distract himself. Since they had arrived at the safe house, he'd had a hell of a time keeping his thoughts on the task at hand.

Dumb, seriously dumb.

He was a murder suspect. This woman might be his only hope of proving his innocence. And still he found himself looking at her as a *woman*.

Blond hair, pretty blue eyes. Petite, but with an athletic frame. He had been surprised to learn she had once worked as a homicide detective. She didn't seem like the type. He would have labeled her a teacher or a counselor. Maybe because of the way she questioned him. He'd had plenty of experience with teachers and counselors.

Merri Walters carried a gun. The teachers and counselors he'd been exposed to as a kid and then a teenager certainly hadn't carried lethal weapons. Unless he counted their ability to prevent his forward movement, academically or otherwise. That was why his folks had opted for homeschooling. Still, outsiders had been involved and there were always difficulties.

He should call his mother and wish her a Merry Christmas, but that would only open the door for questions. He continued to work diligently toward his own goals. As much as he loved his mother, she was one powerfully controlling woman. His father hadn't had a problem with that, but Brandon had. Even as a kid, he'd given her a fit. He needed his freedom to make his own choices. At thirty that shouldn't be an issue. But his mother loved him and she'd been focused solely on him since his father's death three years ago.

Merri wasn't like that. She was smart. Determined and self-sacrificing. He liked her. Wanted to know more about her.

Mostly, he wanted this to be over.

But logic dictated that when the case was over, so would be his connection to her. Be that as it may, he would cross that bridge when he came to it.

Not now.

He eased into the flow of traffic on I-90. Another thirty minutes and they would arrive at their destination. Brandon had been invited to a holiday dinner or two at the Randolph home. Kick's parents liked him, or they had until their son had been murdered and Brandon had become the prime suspect.

They might not be happy to see him under the circumstances. But there was no way around this step. He wished there were. He'd searched his memory for every moment of conversation he and Kick had exchanged the past few months. Truth was, recently they had spent most of their time yelling. Kick was entirely focused on this story, while Brandon worked extended hours to keep a roof over their heads. Kick's failure to pay his share of the rent this month had pushed Brandon over the edge.

But not far enough over to kill the guy.

Next to him, Merri checked the screen of her cell phone. She made a face. "Not a call you care to take, eh?" Being nosey wasn't usually a part of his personality but she made him want to know more… about her.

She glanced at him, blinked. "Excuse me?"

"I was just saying that you apparently didn't want to take that call."

"No." Her lips flattened into a firm line. "That call was a part of my past I'd just as soon forget."

Could mean only one of two things— a former boss or an old lover. "Someone you broke up with?"

Her silence dragged his attention from the road once more. "Didn't mean to get too personal."

The frown that lined her forehead was all too familiar. She looked at him that way a lot. Was there something about him that annoyed her? Maybe she had a headache.

"Let's just say we came to a mutual decision that it was over."

"From your days as a cop?" He wanted to bite his tongue for asking. This was clearly none of his business. But the winter landscape did little to hold his attention. And traffic was sparse since it was Christmas Eve afternoon. Most folks had already arrived at their holiday destinations.

"What?"

He pointed his face in her direction. "The ex-boyfriend. Was he part of your life as a cop?"

"Yes."

Brandon couldn't decide if the frustration in her voice was directed at him or the question. Other than frustration, the pitch of her voice rarely changed. He wished he had that much control over his emotional reactions.

"Why does he still call you?" He should just let it go. But somehow he couldn't.

She'd been staring at him since he'd repeated his last question. Those tiny lines still etched her brow. Maybe she was trying to form a case strategy and just didn't want to talk.

"Because he thinks I'm a traitor."

He sent her a *Really?* look.

"He wanted to move to the next level and I didn't. I came here instead."

"Oh." Lots of baggage and history there. If her former lover was persistent, she could end up with him once more.

"What does *oh* mean?"

Now there was something different. Anger. Another emotion he knew well. "He still wants you." Might as well get to the point.

"Steven Barlow and I are done," she said, her tone simmering with frustration and anger. "He's a great guy, but I can't stand to be smothered. He smothers me."

Now he got it. Merri Walters liked being her own woman. She wasn't about to live or work under anyone else's thumb. Kind of like him.

"Never been married, huh?" He had. In his early twenties he'd fallen madly in love and married within weeks of meeting the girl. Big mistake. Though he liked everything about her, she had one plan: change everything about him. At first he'd tried to make her happy, but then he'd admitted defeat. He was who he was and nothing, except maybe time, was going to change that. She hadn't wanted to wait. According to Kick, Brandon had married his mother.

"I was engaged once," she confessed. "But I fell below the mark where his expectations were concerned and that was the end of that.

She glanced at the screen of her

phone again. This time she opened it and said hello.

Brandon attempted to focus on the road. But he couldn't prevent his ears from listening to every word of the conversation.

"Merry Christmas Eve to you, too, Mom."

The quiet went on for several minutes while Merri repeatedly checked the screen on her phone in between listening to her caller. He could never talk and text at the same time. Good for her. Then she said, "Yes, I'm having a nice holiday. No, I'm not at home."

During the next few minutes, Brandon was relatively certain she spoke to each of her family members. When she finally ended the call, Brandon had surmised that Merri was either the youngest of her clan or she was the one everyone wanted to take care of. And she was fully capable of handling conversation and text simultaneously. She'd done that the entire time on the phone. Maybe she was keeping the agency updated since that Michaels guy had been so concerned for her well being.

Funny, he had the distinct impression that she could take care of herself quite well.

It was quarter past four and near dark as they reached the Blue Island city limits.

"There are a couple of modest motels that we could check out before going to the Randolph home," he suggested. Since he wasn't paying for her services, the least he could do was attempt to keep costs down.

Merri didn't respond. He glanced her way. She was staring at the evolving urban landscape. She never even glanced in his direction.

Maybe she was lost in thought.

He'd noticed that several times already. But it bothered him on some level. Keen senses would be critical to her job.

Rather than touching her, he repeated the question, "Are we planning to stay the night here?"

Merri leaned back in her seat, her gaze focused beyond the front windshield now. Nothing about her posture indicated that she'd heard.

"Merri."

Maybe it was the way he leaned toward her. She jumped as her gaze collided with his. She had been completely zoned out.

"What?" she declared, clearly frustrated.

"You didn't hear me…did you?"

Chapter Seven

Randolph Home, 6:05 p.m.

Merri stepped onto the porch. A large, welcoming wreath decked in Christmas trimmings hung on the door. The electric candles burning in the windows sent a glow of light across the wide porch. Passing by, one would never know that the family inside had suffered a great tragedy. The holiday decor had likely been in place well before the heinous murder.

Brandon waited in the car, both to avoid facing Kick's family and to be able to escape the instant he spotted trouble.

Merri could take care of herself. But if anything—anything at all—seemed fishy, she wanted him out of here. The street in front of the lovely old home had been quiet and clear of vehicles. Those belonging to the homeowners were apparently already secured in garages against the cold Illinois night.

Brandon had let her out on the street behind the Randolph home and he'd parked several houses away on that same back street. She needed him safe. If he hadn't refused to stay at the motel, life would have been much simpler.

WIDELY SPACED STREETLAMPS left all but the sidewalks in near total darkness. Folks in the neighborhood were apparently not concerned about the crime that festered only a few miles away in the big city. Additionally, the few streetlamps allowed the homeowners to observe the stars and prevented too much light from venturing into bedrooms at night.

Merri raised her fist and pounded on the painted wood door. Her purse dragged at her right shoulder. Her parka kept her warm but she would be glad to get inside. The risk that someone was watching remained great no matter how serene the street appeared. For all she knew, trouble could be waiting inside one of the homes. The men who had killed Kick Randolph wouldn't be put off by a little more collateral damage.

The moment she raised her first to knock again, the door opened and the overhead porch light came on. Kick's father, Merri surmised. Tall, like his son, with the same blond hair that had long since turned gray. The pain in his eyes warned that he had no time for solicitors. Yet basic human compassion prevented him from showing any rude tendencies.

"May I help you?"

"Mr. Randolph, my name is Merrilee Walters and I'm from the Colby Agency in Chicago." She pulled out her credentials case and showed her identification. "If you don't mind, I'd like to come inside and speak to you about your son." She didn't add the words *murder* or *homicide*. Mr. Randolph knew full well what had happened to his son.

That aggrieved gaze narrowed with suspicion. "The what agency?"

"Sir, I know this is difficult, but if I could come inside, I'm certain you'll understand that I'm here to help."

He stepped back, pulling the door open wide. "I can't imagine how you believe you can help, but you can come in, I suppose."

Relief flowed along her limbs when the door was closed behind her. Having heard the sounds of a visitor, Mrs. Randolph had come to the entry hall.

"Les, what's going on?" She looked to her husband for explanation. Karen Randolph was tall, like her husband and son, but her blond hair remained so with the aid of chemicals, Merri could tell.

"This woman says she's from the Colby Agency in Chicago and she believes she can help somehow." The man's halfhearted gesture said far more than his words. They had been visited before.

Karen turned to Merri. "Why would you come here at a time like this? Haven't we answered enough questions? The men from that other agency were here for hours this morning. We just need to be left in peace." Tears brimmed on her lashes.

Merri felt horrible for bothering them, but this couldn't wait. Someone else had been here already. "Ma'am, are you referring to the detectives in charge of your son's case?" The woman had said *agency,* but Merri wanted to confirm she'd understood correctly.

Karen shook her head. "The…" she looked to her husband.

"Blackburn Agency," Mr. Randolph said to Merri. "Two men with identification like yours." He nodded at her credential case. "The paper where Kick worked hired them to look into...the case."

Merri couldn't be sure whether the *Trib* had hired someone or not, but Simon could check it out. "Do you mind if I call my superior and ask him to verify that the Blackburn Agency has been retained by the *Tribune?*"

The couple exchanged a look, then settled their collective attention on Merri once more. The husband said, "I can't see any harm in that, but, are you implying that the men who were here today weren't hired by the *Trib?*"

The fear that glinted in the mother's eyes tore at Merri's heart.

"Sir, I'm not suggesting anything at this point. What I am trying to do is to make sure that I'm not unnecessarily repeating another party's efforts." That should assuage their misgivings for the moment.

"Certainly then," Randolph agreed. "We would very much like confirmation."

"Why…" Karen took a steadying breath. "Why don't you come into the living room and sit down."

Merri was thankful for her hospitality. "That would be very nice."

As soon as she'd taken a seat directly across from the Randolphs' position on the sofa, she sent a text to Simon. He would call when he had an answer.

"…your agency?"

Merri's gaze zeroed in on Mr. Randolph's face. "I'm sorry, sir, you'll have to wait until I'm looking at you to speak." *Just say it!* "I read lips."

Why couldn't she just say that to Brandon? Vanity, pure and simple. She didn't want him to see her that way.

"Oh." Mr. Randolph glanced at his wife, then settled his full attention on Merri. "I was asking who retained your agency."

That was one answer she couldn't give him. "The Colby Agency is working with the official investigation." It wasn't exactly true, but it wasn't a lie, either. "We're trying to get to the bottom of exactly what happened."

The conversation turned to Brandon. Neither of Kick's parents could believe Brandon capable of such a thing, but their son's death was far too painful at the moment to truly rule out Brandon as a suspect. They needed the facts, for the peace of all concerned.

"Would you mind going over with me what the men who were here earlier wanted to know?"

Kick's mother spoke first. "They wanted to know about the story Kevin was working on. We knew it was something big, but he refused to discuss anything about it. So we couldn't help."

The exhaustion and misery had deepened and darkened around her eyes, giving her already pale complexion a deathly pallor.

"I know just how difficult this is," Merri qualified, "but it would help tremendously if you could tell me as much as possible about your son's life here at home. School. Friends."

The two exchanged another look. The father spoke this time. "The Blackburn investigators asked those same questions."

Not surprising. "Do you mind going over those painful elements once more?"

Merri's cell vibrated. "Excuse me one moment. This is my superior." She opened the phone. "Walters." She read the text her screen provided as Simon spoke, relating that the *Trib* insisted they were leaving the investigation up to the experts—Chicago PD. They insisted they had not hired anyone.

As she closed the phone, she considered the best way to relay this information. These folks had been hurt enough already. But they needed the truth.

"Ma'am, sir," she said to them, "the *Tribune* insists they are leaving the investigation to Chicago PD."

She quickly wrote the name and number of the man Simon had contacted on one of her business cards and placed it on the table between them. "If you want to confirm that information, please call this gentleman. My number is there as well if you have any questions after I'm gone."

"You're saying those men were…" Mr. Randolph fell silent.

"Your son," Merri began, "was working on a big story that may have rattled some cages. Powerful cages. If that's the case, and I believe it is, you should protect yourselves. Check in with the detective in charge of the case whenever anyone shows up with questions."

"Then," Mrs. Randolph said, "you won't mind if we call Detective Whitehall and ask about you."

"Of course not." The Colby Agency maintained an outstanding relationship with Chicago PD. Simon had already discussed Merri's involvement with the detective. "We'll all feel more comfortable if you verify why I'm here and what I've told you."

Mr. Randolph stood. "I'll give the detective a call."

When he'd left the room, his wife turned to Merri. "Do you believe, based on what you know, that Brandon killed Kick?" The misery on her face spoke volumes about her fear that her son may have trusted a man capable of such heinousness.

"No, ma'am," Merri said honestly. "I don't believe that at all. There is a concerted effort to gain access to evidence related to the story your son was working on. I believe Brandon Thomas is a scapegoat, as well as the only connection whoever is doing this feels they have to the evidence."

Karen Randolph closed her eyes a moment, then opened them to Merri once more. "Thank you. I need to hang on to that. My son is dead, whoever killed him. But the idea that his roommate…his best friend…" She shook her head. "I can't get right with that."

Merri was glad to have confirmation that her instincts were right on target.

"What did you discuss with the other men?" Merri asked.

"They wanted to see his room. If he had any special secret places where he might hide something relevant to what he was working on."

Even his own family had no idea what he was up to. For their own protection, Merri presumed.

"We had no knowledge of his work, other than the articles that made it into the paper." Karen shrugged. "And if he ever had a secret place where he might hide things, we never knew about it."

"Did he have any friends in the neighborhood? Maybe someone he attended school with? Someone he was particularly close to?"

Again, Karen shook her head. "He wasn't the athletic type, so he never did sports. He didn't join any clubs. He had a couple of sort-of friends back in high school, but they've all moved away. I can't imagine that he would have contacted any of them. But I'll be glad to give you names if you'd like."

Merri wasn't sure she would need them, but better to err on the side of caution. "That could prove helpful as we go along."

"Would you like to see his room?" The hopeful expression in her eyes told Merri that Karen was looking for an excuse to talk about her son…to show off his things.

"Yes, please."

Karen rose and headed for the stairs in the entry hall. Merri did the same. Lester Randolph met them at the bottom of the stairs.

An alarm sounded deep inside Merri. If possible, the pain had deepened on the man's face.

"I spoke to Detective Whitehall," he said to Merri. Then turning to his wife, he continued, "The Colby Agency is looking into the case. They were retained by Brandon Thomas."

For one long trauma-filled moment Merri feared that would be the end of her visit.

Merri knew that Mrs. Randolph spoke but since her back was turned, she couldn't read the words on her lips.

"I know how you feel about that," Randolph said to his wife, "I didn't say I thought it was true. I just—" his gaze lit on Merri "—want the truth."

"Mr. Randolph—" Merri acknowledged him, then his wife when she turned back to her "—Mrs. Randolph, I wasn't trying to mislead you in any way. I certainly wouldn't have suggested you call the detective if I'd planned on deceiving you. I didn't mention that Brandon was involved with this investigation because I didn't want to add to your suffering in any way."

The two stared at her for a time. Mrs. Randolph broke the ice first. "I don't care who you're working for as long as it's the truth you're seeking."

Merri gave her a nod of assurance. "You have my word and my agency's word. Feel free to call me or the office any time. This is about the truth. Yes, I'd like nothing better than to prove my client's innocence, but the bottom line is the truth. Detective Whitehall will be appraised of all my findings."

"That's all we can ask for." Mr. Randolph led the way to his son's room.

Merri followed his wife.

The first door on the right led to Kick's room, which faced the street side of the property. The walls were white. The furnishings were oak. Beige carpet. No posters, no trophies. A few books on the shelves. No personality whatsoever.

Except for the ancient computer sitting atop a desk in the corner. Even then, this wasn't what she would have expected from an aspiring journalist.

"Is the room similar to the way he left

it when he went away to college?" She wanted to ask were these the things that marked the room as Kick's, but she hadn't wanted to say it exactly that way.

"This is exactly the way it's always been. We've painted the walls a couple of times but he always wanted it white."

Unexpected.

Together they went through the drawers and the closet, which were mostly bare. The few CDs he'd left behind were without cases. Nothing in the pockets of the few items of clothing in the closet. Nothing under the bed or mattress. The only items that gave any indication that he'd ever lived here was the computer and his senior yearbook.

While Mr. Randolph powered up the computer, Mrs. Randolph covered the highlights of the yearbook. Nothing there, either. The guy hadn't belonged to anything. There were two pictures of him in the yearbook. His senior portrait and a class photo.

"There's nothing on the computer's hard drive," his father said. "It's as if when he finished with it he wiped it clean."

The father was correct. The computer held nothing but the original software installed.

"What about his sister?"

"Bethany is at home with her family," Mrs. Randolph put in quickly.

"It is Christmas Eve," Mr. Randolph added. "And she has small children."

Perfectly logical explanation. But Merri needed to speak to the sister.

"If you think of anything else or if anyone who makes you uncomfortable comes around," Merri urged, "call me. You have my number on that card."

Mr. Randolph moved toward the window. Mrs. Randolph turned that way, as well. The two had a brief exchange, but Merri only picked up bits and pieces.

"What's happening?" she asked, her instincts screaming a warning.

Mr. Randolph frowned. "Someone in the street is blowing the horn. Don't they know that it's late?"

Merri rushed to the window. Verified as the vehicle rolled beneath a streetlight that it was Simon's sedan moving slowly down the street. "Is that the car making the noise?"

"I believe so," Randolph said.

"I have to go." Merri thrust out her hand. "Thank you so much for your help." She started backing out of the room. "I'll call you."

She rushed down the stairs. Wasn't sure whether she dared go out the front. Instead, she rushed through the kitchen and out the back door. She couldn't hear the horn blowing, but Brandon wouldn't have known that.

She spotted a car moving slowly down the street in front of the house where he'd dropped her off.

Merri sprinted across the Randolphs' yard and then the one behind that. The streetlamp he passed under allowed her to once more identify Simon's car.

It was definitely Brandon.

She raced to the street.

The car squealed to a stop.

She'd jumped into the passenger seat before it completely stopped rocking. "What's going on?"

Brandon turned to her. "A dark sedan, four doors, three men. Drove past the Randolph house four times. Then they didn't come back."

Damn it. "They may have parked somewhere to come back on foot and check things out. They must have a spotter watching the house." She pressed him with her gaze. "They know we're here."

Headlights cut through the darkness behind them.

Brandon stomped the accelerator.

Merri was thankful he didn't need directions.

There was only one thing to do at this point…

Clear out.

Brandon skidded into a right turn, then a sharp left.

He'd been here before. Surely he knew the most efficient route for losing a tail.

Merri slid her safety belt across her torso and snapped it into place as the vehicle bolted forward.

Brandon slammed the brakes and took a hard left at the next intersection.

She twisted at the waist, tried to see what was behind them.

The rear windshield cracked right before her eyes. A web of lines split from the crack.

A gunshot!

Brandon flattened a palm against her head and pushed her down into the seat. The safety belt cut into her neck.

Merri grappled for the weapon in her purse. The way the car was fishtailing and skidding, she dropped the gun twice before she got a firm grip on it.

She raised her torso upward. He

shoved her down again. She glared at him. His lips were moving but his face was turned away toward the street. What the hell was he saying?

Another high-velocity turn, then he rammed his foot against the accelerator and the vehicle charged forward. Every time she tried to rise up, he pushed her back down. She was a highly trained investigator, a former cop. What the hell was he doing?

A lunge to the right and then an abrupt stop.

Headlights went off. Brandon slammed the gearshift into Park and turned the key in the ignition to the off position as the car rocked one last time.

Total darkness.

Brandon didn't move.

Merri didn't dare move.

A long minute passed with no movement. No light. Nothing.

Then the pressure on her head and

shoulder eased and he allowed her to sit upright.

It was dark as pitch.

She couldn't see enough of his face to read his lips but she understood the universal gesture to remain quiet. He held his finger to his lips, then to hers. Despite the circumstances, a spear of warmth shot through her body.

Another minute, maybe two passed with no movement, no light and utter stillness. Then he slid down in the seat until his head was lower than the back of it, ensuring no one could see him. Merri did the same. He took her cell phone and held it open so that the light from the screen would illuminate his face.

It wasn't until that moment that she considered that he didn't have his cell phone on him. The police had taken it along with his wallet and apparently not returned it. No wonder he hadn't been able to call her when she was in the Randolphs' house.

His lips moved and she peered intently to recognize the words.

"We're safe here. They won't see us."

She didn't know precisely where they were, but she had to trust him.

"Don't move. Don't talk," he warned, his expression unyielding. "If we're completely still, we'll be okay until the coast is clear."

Merri told herself to relax. They were safe.

For now.

Chapter Eight

Christmas Day, 4:48 a.m.

It was still dark.

And it was cold as hell.

They had waited quietly for hours last night. The winter chill had invaded the vehicle. But between their coats and, more important, the warmth of their bodies they had managed to stay warm. At some point they had both fallen asleep. Merri wasn't sure if she'd surrendered to the weariness first or if he had.

Whatever the case, she'd slept like the dead. Even better than she had at the lake house yesterday morning. Had to be the man holding her tightly against him…as if he were afraid she would suddenly disappear.

Brandon appeared to be asleep even now.

It was still too dark to see his face, but Merri confirmed her conclusion by the rise and fall of his muscled chest. After she'd fallen asleep, she'd somehow managed to make a pillow out of his torso. He felt strong, and warm. She'd snuggled deeper inside his coat, pressing her face to his sweater—the only thing separating her cheek from his chest. Her legs cramped in their curled-up position along the length of the front seat. Brandon's were stretched out in the floorboard all the way across to her side of the vehicle.

If she wasn't careful in moving up and away from the draw of his warmth, she would encounter the steering wheel. But she had to move. She couldn't let him wake up and find her sprawled across his body like this.

Any way she moved, there was no way to avoid a part of him stretched out that way.

She scooted her backside as close to the passenger door as possible as she pulled up, grasping the back of the seat for leverage. If she could just find the door handle, she didn't care if she fell out of the car. Right now, she had to remove herself from this compromising position before he woke up and noticed.

Her fingers wrapped around the handle and yanked. The door moved. So did Merri. She scrambled, righting herself, until her feet were on the ground. She swayed upward. Careful not to make any more noise than she already had, she eased the door closed and tried to survey their surroundings.

Merri stumbled around the car. They were in a driveway of some sort. There was a house…as best she could see in the darkness. The canopy of trees didn't allow the meager light from the stars and the streetlamps to filter through.

Taking care, she moved toward the edge of the yard and peeked past the thick shrubs that towered well over her head. The street was deserted. The streetlamp on the corner provided sufficient light for her to see that the coast appeared to be clear.

Their tail had given up on the chase.

She breathed a sigh of relief. They could leave. Go back to the motel and…

A hand settled on her shoulder. She jumped. Barely bit back a squeak.

His scent told her it was Brandon before her eyes took in and registered his frame in the deep gloom.

He said something but she couldn't see well enough in the near darkness to comprehend the words.

Taking her hand in his, he led her back to the car. She shouldn't have noticed how the warm feel of his palm sent a shiver along her arm. Or that the smell of him had completely invaded her lungs and had her pulse thumping faster. She would have much preferred blaming the physical reaction on the scare he'd given her, but she understood that wasn't the problem.

That silly attraction she'd noted before was playing havoc with her ability to remain neutral toward the man who was her client. Her *first* client. Not a good thing at all. She had to get a handle on her professionalism.

He opened the passenger side door for her, she slid into the seat. Thankfully the interior light didn't come on when the door was opened. Obviously Simon or Brandon had recently set the interior lamp to the Off position, which was good because someone could be watching from a position she hadn't detected on the street.

Brandon moved around the hood and settled behind the steering wheel, then fiddled with the controls until the interior light came on.

Before she could protest, he turned to her and said, "We have to talk. This can't wait."

Several things flashed through her mind as he said the words. Him pushing her down in the seat during the car chase. His holding her there until they were safely away from the threat. Then, him holding his finger to his lips then hers…and using the light from her cell phone to ensure she could see when he spoke to her.

He knew.

"You should have told me." Those dark eyes were impossible to read with any certainty. But she understood from the expression on his face that he was not happy.

"It's not something I find easy to admit right up front." She hadn't had any trouble explaining her situation to the Randolphs. But that was different. Brandon was her client. She wanted him to feel confident in her ability.

And he was a man to whom she felt some physical attraction, like it or not.

"You can't hear anything at all."

That the disappointment or whatever she'd seen turned into worry shouldn't have given her such a warm, fuzzy feeling just then, but it did. She shook her head. "Though I do remember what things sound like." When she wanted to take the time, she could conjure up the sounds in her mind related to any activity she'd done in the past. She didn't do that as much anymore. She'd gotten used to the silence. Operating in that mode felt normal, instinctive. Strange, she mused, how the human body adapted to whatever circumstances became necessary.

"You read lips extraordinarily well."

The teachers and experts she'd sought out at first had been amazed by her lip-reading. She'd done some of that, she'd realized eventually, her entire life. Watching people had always been her favorite pastime. She hadn't meant to eavesdrop on anyone's conversation, but she had occasionally. Honing that skill had been part of the natural evolution after she'd lost her ability to hear. Ultimately she'd done what she had to do to survive. The same way a person who'd lost a limb learned to overcome that challenge. End of story.

"I didn't like the business of sign language," she admitted. Though it was a great communication method for some, she didn't go for it. Mainly, she supposed, because that was a blatant admission to any and all that she couldn't hear. She'd wrestled with the question as to whether she didn't want people to know because it indicated a physical weakness or because she wanted to prove she was just as capable as anyone who still possessed their hearing.

Bottom line: she'd been denying that her life was different for several years now.

"So there was a time when you could hear."

She nodded. "Until I was into my twenties."

"What happened?" He searched her eyes. "If you don't mind sharing that with me."

The answer to that question was still a little cloudy. "It was one of the bizarre infections the medical professionals couldn't find a way to treat. When I was finally well again, I couldn't hear. I tried a couple of surgical procedures but neither one worked. It seemed smarter to go on with my life and just attempt to live with the situation."

He reached out. She braced. His fingers traced her left ear. The anticipation of feeling those fingertips on her mouth had her catching her breath. As if he'd read her mind, he made a path with those long fingers along the line of her jaw to her mouth before he let his hand fall away. The intent expression on his face tightened her chest. She liked having him touch her.

"I noticed you'd missed a couple of

things I said," he explained, "but it wasn't obvious until we were running from those men. I shouted for you to get down when the first shot rang out but you didn't hear me."

He'd pushed her down in the seat when she didn't listen. He'd saved both their lives by losing that tail. He'd saved her by thinking quickly. "Thank you for getting us out of that situation."

"I need coffee."

There it was. She saw it even as he turned away and started the car.

He looked at her differently now.

No one ever saw her the same way after they found out.

Brandon would be no exception, even though she was pretty sure he struggled with a challenge of his own. One he'd managed to set aside quite well during that intense chase. She didn't understand that part.

Men…they were the worst at accepting flaws.

5:30 a.m.

"THEY'LL BE LOOKING for this car."

"If we're lucky," Merri said as they braked to a stop at an intersection near their destination, "they won't be out this early." She looked around the neighborhood. "We need to visit Kick's sister, but it's a little early for that, too."

Brandon sat at the intersection a moment, his foot on the brake so the car wouldn't move forward. He needed to get his bearings, and it wasn't daylight. He turned to Merri. "Bethany lives a few streets over." But Merri was right; it was early and he needed coffee badly. "There's a church—"

"What?"

Damn. He'd momentarily forgotten that she needed to see his lips. He turned his face toward hers. "There's a church a couple of blocks from Bethany's house. We could wait it out there."

"Sounds workable."

Kick had taken Brandon to that church once or twice. The doors stayed open 24/7 so people could come in and pray whenever they wanted. Brandon hoped that hadn't changed since he'd been here last.

Keeping an eye out for other vehicles, he drove the short distance. The church parking lot was empty as he'd known it would be. Instead of pulling into the lot, he drove past it and parked on a side street. If the bastards after them spotted this car, they would surely descend upon the church. Brandon might not get so lucky the next time they gave chase. His ability to react hadn't been delayed...*that time*.

He tapped Merri on the shoulder so she would look at him and said, "We can walk to the church from here. Then when we're ready to go to Bethany's house, it's within walking distance also."

"They'll be watching her house."

True. He wasn't sure what the best course of action was to avoid that scenario. Maybe Merri would have some ideas. Right now he needed that coffee.

He took a route across several back lawns, finally approaching the church from the rear. The back door was locked. Worry inched up his spine. Thankfully, the front entrance opened without hesitation. A church bulletin stuck on one door announced that Christmas mass would be from eight until eleven a.m. that day.

Inside, he led the way through the vestibule to the main sanctuary. Dim lights highlighted the altar area where a kneeling bar waited for those who sought to bow down before the massive cross.

Instead of going to the altar, he weaved his way around it and to the rooms in the rear.

Merri tugged on his hand, and he turned to face her.

"Where are we going?"

He hitched his head toward the narrow hall beyond the door to his right. "Bathrooms and a kitchen are back this way."

Her expression brightened. "Great."

In the hall, she disappeared into the ladies' room while he headed for the kitchen. He went through the cabinets until he found what he'd hoped for: coffee and filters. When he had a pot brewing, he made a path for the men's room. He passed Merri en route. "The coffee's brewing," he said to her.

She'd washed her face and finger-combed her hair, but she still looked rumpled and as sexy as hell. He resisted the urge to smile. Merri Walters looked damn good in the mornings. No matter under what conditions she had spent the night.

When he'd taken care of personal business he hesitated at the sink. How could his life have gone downhill so far so quickly? He stared at his reflection and wondered how anyone could believe him to be a murderer. As angry as he often got at Kick, he would never have done anything like that. The knucklehead was like a brother to him. Otherwise, Brandon would have gotten a new roommate years ago. This was all way too insane.

He threaded his fingers through his hair, didn't care if it looked tousled. Brandon had never tried to be the spit-and-polish type. He couldn't care less.

Until now. Somehow it was important on a level he didn't fully understand that Merri thought the best of him. That she liked him.

"Dumb, Brandon."

When he joined her in the kitchen she'd located two mugs and poured warm brew into each.

"I couldn't find any cream."

He didn't care. "Thanks." He downed a gulp of the hot liquid. Warm, tasty. Felt good just knowing that the caffeine would soon infuse his veins. He needed a jolt this morning. Sleeping with her practically on top of him, the uncomfortable circumstances not withstanding, had been seriously difficult. His body had tightened and rushed toward arousal with no way to slow it down. She'd felt good against him. Her weight…her warmth. And, God, her shape. He'd wanted to run his hands over every part of her body, but he hadn't dared cross that line.

The woman was armed, after all.

As they sipped a second cup of coffee more slowly, Merri broached the subject he had dreaded. "How old were you when your dyslexia was diagnosed?"

Like her, he didn't exactly go around broadcasting the fact that he was dyslexic. He'd expected her to figure it out. "Ten."

"Your teachers didn't notice before then?"

"My mother was my teacher," he explained. "I was homeschooled."

Merri nodded, the expression on her face showing her disapproval.

"Public schools can be problematic."

She set her cup on the counter. "Tell

me about it. I taught elementary school for a couple of years. Problematic is putting it mildly."

He'd known it! "I thought you'd been a teacher at some point."

Her eyebrows formed a vee, creating the cutest image of surprise. "How did you know that? I told you I used to be a cop."

"The way you rephrased your questions when you quizzed me back at the apartment." He poured himself a third cup, then realized the pot was empty. He motioned to her cup. She shook her head so he set the carafe back on the warmer and turned the machine off. "You recognized that you weren't getting through to me so you rephrased the question until I caught on."

She smiled. He liked when she smiled. She looked soft and sweet…and womanly. "I saw the clues but I couldn't be sure. Usually by the mid-twenties, it's not an obvious problem."

It generally wasn't. "I seem to fall back

into my old patterns when I'm stressed." And he'd definitely been stressed the past forty-eight hours.

"Understandable." She inclined her head and studied him. "That's probably typical. I just haven't had that much experience with the adult side of the problem. You can't recall events in proper sequence. Things get jumbled up. There's a delayed reaction in physical and mental responses."

He nodded. Like all the things he should remember that Kick had said to him, he didn't. But the murder and everything since had churned things up. He couldn't retrieve the information in any kind of decent order. Some things he couldn't seem to pull from his brain at all.

The clock on the wall indicated that it was close to seven. "Since it's Christmas morning, Bethany's likely up by now." Her kids would never allow her to sleep late on this day. "We could head that way." According to what Merri had told him last night she hadn't learned much from Kick's parents—except that two men pretending to represent another P.I. agency had questioned the couple. Merri had warned them to beware. Their ignorance had likely been the reason they had survived the encounter without being tortured or killed.

"Since Kick's parents don't consider you a real suspect," Merri offered, "we can assume the sister might not. That could prove to our advantage."

"She won't." Brandon knew Bethany would never believe he was a suspect.

Merri pulled her coat closer around her and shifted the purse strap on her shoulder. "Lead the way. I'll follow."

Brandon cleaned up the mess they'd made first, then led the way outside. He chose his route carefully. Through more yards. Most were decorated for Christmas with snowmen and Santas. Sleighs and reindeer. Lots of twinkling lights that had come on since they'd taken refuge in the church. Beyond some of the windows he saw families gathered around the trees opening presents. Not one suspected the trouble right outside their home.

Life had once been like that for Brandon. Before he'd decided his mother was hampering his life. She worried so about him. She sheltered him entirely too much. He'd dated, had a few girlfriends. Even married at a really young age. But none of those women had connected with him.

None ever understood his challenge. He couldn't always react the way he should. And every time he screwed up, he paid the price.

A private college had given him the skills he needed to survive in the world of architectural engineering. He'd learned that he worked better alone and on his own. Private contracting had served him well. He worked from home more often than not. By the time this was over, he would be behind, but a few all-nighters and he would be caught up.

If this was ever over.

He still refused to believe that the justice system would put him behind bars for a murder he hadn't committed. To hedge his bets he'd gone to the Colby Agency. He glanced at the woman at his side. He'd made the right choice on more levels than one.

At Bethany Stover's kitchen door, Brandon approached with caution. The lights were on, and he could smell breakfast. Brandon's stomach rumbled as he peered through the window of the door.

He could imagine Bethany, her husband and two kids gathered around the Christmas tree in the family room. He and Merri might be forced to wait a while longer before interrupting that wondrous event but—

Bethany, flannel gown flowing to the floor, entered the kitchen. She, at least, was up and about and not already too deeply entrenched in the Christmas tradition.

Merri knocked on the door before Brandon had a chance to properly brace for the reunion.

Startled, Bethany turned toward the door. Since it was dark on the stoop beyond the door, she shuffled across the room and flipped the switch. Brandon waved to her and she blinked, startled all over again.

The hesitation lasted only a few seconds, but her reaction to seeing him was mixed. Still, she unlocked and opened the door.

"Brandon?" She glanced at Merri. "What're you doing here?"

"Hey, Bethany." Brandon didn't move to step inside. Not until he was invited… or more certain of her feelings. "I know it's not a good time, considering what's happened and the fact that it's Christmas morning, but we need to talk."

Another second's hesitation and Bethany stepped back far enough to allow them in. "I guess it's okay. The kids and Larry are still asleep."

As Brandon and Merri moved past her, she added, "We haven't gotten a lot of sleep the past couple of nights."

She didn't have to explain. Her brother was dead. Brandon was supposed to be his best friend. Instead he was a person of interest in his murder.

"I'm really sorry about what happened," Brandon said.

"My parents told me about what you'd done. I understand you're trying to help." She looked to Merri. "Have you learned anything yet?"

"Considering," Merri said carefully, "what I've experienced since taking Brandon as a client, I'd have to say he's telling the truth—if you're asking me whether or not I believe he's innocent."

Bethany gestured to the table. "Have a seat."

When they'd settled around the table, Kick's sister added, "I never considered you a suspect." This she said to Brandon. "I knew something was wrong. I just didn't know what. I couldn't understand why I hadn't been able to contact you." She studied his face. "Are you all right? The police called and told us about the apartment. It's all just horrible and doesn't seem to end." Her eyes glistened with emotion.

He still had trouble accepting that Kick was dead and that he had no home. "I'm okay. I just want to stop these guys. I want whoever's responsible for Kick's murder brought to justice."

Bethany nodded. "I'm hoping that happens, too, but I don't want you caught up in this. Why don't you let the police handle it? You could go into hiding if the men who hurt Kick are after you, too." She meant what she said. Her eyes told him that they'd come from the heart.

Merri shook her head, drawing the woman's attention back to her. "It won't be that easy. Whoever hired these men wants the evidence your brother had in his possession. They're not going to stop until they find it or the man who hired them is revealed so the police can deal with him. It may get even uglier."

Bethany shook her head. "If you came here because you think I know something." She gave her head another shake. "I don't know anything. Kick talked about working on a big story the last time he was here." Tears glimmered in her already puffy eyes. "He wouldn't say a word. Not a word. Except that it was big and someone was going down. Someone important to the city of Chicago."

"You think," Brandon suggested, "this person might have been a politician? A high-level member of law enforcement? Something like that?"

"I wish I could help you, but I just don't know." She glanced longingly at the coffeemaker. "Why don't I make us some coffee?"

Brandon didn't mention that they'd

already had coffee. He imagined it made Bethany feel somewhat more in control to do something.

When she'd poured the coffee, she brought a tray to the table and passed out the mugs. "Would you like pancakes? They're hot off the griddle?"

Merri shook her head, then offered, "There is one way you could help us."

Bethany settled in her chair and cradled her mug. "Name it."

"Kick gave Brandon some random clues to finding where he'd hidden the evidence these men are looking for. But we haven't been able to make a lot of sense of the phrases yet."

Bethany stopped mid-sip of her coffee and looked at Brandon.

"It may be nothing," Brandon said, not wanting her to get her hopes up. "But we do believe the phrases indicate that he left something here, in his hometown. But that's as far as we've gotten."

"The part we haven't figured out,"

Merri put in before Bethany could ask questions, "is the final clue: *Invisible.*"

Bethany's face went pale. "Invisible?"

Merri nodded. "Does that mean something to you?"

Brandon had considered the word a dozen ways and other than that the item was well hidden, he couldn't fathom what Kick meant by the term.

"Back in high school," Bethany clarified, "Kick wasn't the guy he is—was—more recently." To Brandon, she said, "By the time you met him, he'd become Kick Randolph, the man with a plan to make it all the way to the top of his field." She sighed, stared into her cup. "But back in high school he was a total introvert. No friends to speak of. He didn't play any sports, wasn't in the band. He was nobody. That's what the kids who liked to make fun of him called him. It was awful for him." A tear slid down her cheek, she swiped at it with the back of her hand. "His senior year he was given a trophy by those snotty cheerleaders he'd gone to school with for four years."

"A trophy?" Merri repeated.

Bethany nodded as she swiped away more of those tears. "Mr. Invisible. That's what they dubbed him. The guy in their graduating class most likely to spend the rest of his life being *unseen*."

Invisible. That had to be it. "That explains the term." Brandon clenched his fists beneath the table. Now he understood why Kick would always boast about the fact that he understood how Brandon felt about his dyslexia. He'd suffered, too. Why the hell hadn't he ever told Brandon the whole story?

Didn't matter now. What mattered was finding the truth. "The evidence he had hidden would be on some sort of storage device," Brandon described. "Does the word *invisible* give you any idea where he might have hidden a video or some kind of electronic storage device?"

Bethany started to shake her head no,

but then she stopped. "Wait. There was a trophy." She frowned in concentration. "At the high school." Insight replaced some of the emotion still glistening in her eyes. "They gave him a trophy on Awards Day. The principal was so appalled at what his classmates did, he stuck it away in some storage room." A slight smile tilted her lips. "But when Kick started making a name for himself in Chicago, the principal pulled out that old trophy and put it in the display case with all the other ones. You know, all the state championship ones. Kind of an in-your-face move since a lot of my brother's old classmates still live around here."

"You believe it's possible the trophy may provide some insight into where he hid the evidence," Merri suggested, her face hopeful.

Bethany nodded. "That has to be it. That's the only thing that comes to mind. Kick was pretty proud of what the principal had done."

"How does a guy so invisible during school get a nickname like Kick?" Merri asked.

Brandon could understand how she would wonder. Now that he knew the whole story, he wondered, as well.

Bethany made another of those exasperated sounds. "He used to hate the nickname since it was about him being the guy everyone could *kick* around. But after he moved to Chicago and started garnering a few kudos in his career, he liked the sort of inside distinction."

"There's one more thing," Merri said, breaking the silence that had fallen over Brandon and Bethany. "The men who questioned your parents will come to you next, most likely. You cannot share any of this with them. They can't know we've been here. If they press you by saying they know we were here, tell them that you kicked us out because you're angry with Brandon."

"I understand." Another frown marred

Bethany's brow. "What're you going to do?"

Merri got to her feet and pushed in her chair. "We're going to find that evidence and ensure justice is done for Kick and for Brandon."

It took some persuading to get Bethany to go along with the idea that they had to go back out there and do this alone. But she insisted Merri and Brandon use her minivan. Brandon didn't argue. The car they had been in was damaged and would be recognizable by the bad guys. They needed to keep as low a profile as possible.

Equally helpful, Bethany had given them the key to the school. Her husband was a math teacher at the high school as well as a coach. If they were lucky, her husband would never know he'd facilitated an illegal entry of school property.

Again Brandon drove, since he knew the neighborhood.

Bethany had also insisted they wear different clothes. The fit wasn't so great, but it would work. The ski hats and change of coats provided the best disguises.

Now all they had to do was break into the high school without getting caught.

On Christmas.

Chapter Nine

Chicago, Home of Victoria Colby-Camp, 8:30 a.m.

Victoria Colby-Camp slipped her arms into her coat and smiled as her husband smoothed the heavy wool over her shoulders. She and Lucas were nearing their sixth anniversary, and life could not be better.

Their granddaughter was safely at home with her parents enjoying Christmas after the harrowing scare by the thugs who would have kidnapped her this past summer had Victoria and the entire Colby agency not intervened. Jim,

Victoria's son, and his wife Tasha were happier than ever with a second child on the way. The scare of the last ill-fated pregnancy was well behind them as this pregnancy moved into the second trimester.

Things at the Colby Agency were running more smoothly than ever.

Life was good.

The Colby family had fought evil and triumphed once more.

The telephone rang and Victoria paused at the door.

"We're going to be late," Lucas suggested, knowing his wife couldn't resist answering the call.

"It could be Jim," she allowed by way of an excuse, even though Jim would call her cell phone if he needed to reach her.

"That's not entirely impossible," Lucas offered with a knowing smile.

Victoria laughed as she made her way to where the phone sat on the side table next to the door. She answered, expecting to hear Simon's or Ian's voice. Either one could be calling to be the first to wish her a good Christmas morning.

"Victoria," the unfamiliar voice said, "this is Clive Mathias. I apologize for calling you so early on this auspicious day, but I have an urgent matter to discuss that involves both of us."

A frown spread its way across Victoria's brow as the identity of the caller nudged its way through her distraction. "Good morning, Clive. How can I help you?" She shrugged in question at her husband who looked equally confounded.

"I've become aware that an investigator of yours is hindering a homicide investigation."

Now Victoria was really confused. "I'm afraid you have me at a loss." Of course, she was aware that the investigation of which he spoke was no doubt the Randolph case. What she could not fathom was why Clive Mathias, the head of Chicago's Crime Commission, would feel compelled to call and discuss the investigation.

"You're aware," Mathias went on, "that your investigator, Merrilee Walters, is looking into the Randolph homicide."

"Well aware," Victoria returned. "Is there a problem with how the investigation is being handled? It was my impression that Ms. Walters intends to cooperate with Detective Whitehall in the event she learns anything of significance to the case."

"The problem appears to be your investigator's inability to maintain any manner of control over her actions and their repercussions. I'm afraid she's making us both look rather bad."

The suggestion riled Victoria. "Again, I have no idea what you mean, Clive." To Victoria's knowledge, Merri hadn't called in last night or this morning, but she was well within her twenty-four-hour period of being incommunicado. There was absolutely no reason to be concerned yet.

"Ms. Walters has taken a person of interest out of our jurisdiction where he continues to be out of reach. It's my understanding that after visiting the family of the deceased there was some disruption of the peace in a nearby neighborhood."

This was all news to Victoria. "I can assure you, Clive, that I will look into the situation. If Ms. Walters has overstepped the bounds of her position as an investigator on my staff, appropriate measures will be taken." Victoria knew without question that the suggestion was ludicrous.

"Mr. Thomas should be returned to this jurisdiction immediately, Victoria. He should not be causing distress for the family of a murder victim. I'm certain you understand how difficult things could become if this gets out of hand."

Victoria assured the man that she would attend to the matter straight away. When she had replaced the handset in the charger stand, she turned to her husband. "Something's happened with Merri."

Lucas nodded. "Then you need to deal with the issue."

As they drove to her son's house, Victoria discussed the strange communication with Ian and Simon via a three-way call. Neither of her seconds-in-command had heard from Merri since the afternoon before.

"I'll keep trying to get through to Merri's cell," Simon suggested. "If I don't connect with her in the next two hours, I will personally look into the situation in Blue Island."

As much as Victoria hated to disrupt Simon's holiday, verifying Merri's well-being was essential.

"My question," Ian chimed in, "is what does Mathias have to do with this?"

Victoria agreed wholeheartedly. Clive Mathias rarely got involved with day-to-day operations. Particularly with a fairly low-level investigation—not that any murder was actually low-level. But Kevin Randolph was no one important to Chicago politics or society. Mathias rarely delved into anything less than a "high-profile" case. He had underlings for the "regular" work.

"I would like to know the answer to that one myself, Ian." Victoria was thankful Ian didn't proclaim this instance as a perfect example of Merri's inability to handle an investigation alone.

"We'll take care of this, Victoria," Simon urged. "Enjoy your holiday with the family. If there's anything you need to know, we'll pass it along."

For more than two decades, Victoria had maintained the helm at the Colby Agency. Now, she was more than happy to have her two most trusted associates take care of business for her.

She deserved this time with her family.

Merri Walters knew what she was doing. If she needed backup, Ian and Simon would see that she got exactly that. Clive Mathis had no reason to worry.

Merri wouldn't let the Colby Agency or Chicago PD down.

Chapter Ten

Chicago, 9:00 a.m.

"I don't care what you have to do," Clive Mathias told his detective, "you get this situation under control."

The silence that emanated from the other end of the line warned Clive that Detective Whitehall was out of his league.

Finally the other man said, "Sir, I'm doing my best but this *situation* is totally out of control. I can't—"

"Just take care of it," Clive almost shouted. "It's Christmas, for God's sake, man. You know what to do. Just do it."

Clive disconnected. He had nothing more to say. Whitehall would regain control or else.

This was totally unacceptable. No one as pointless as Kevin Randolph, much less his inept friend, was going to ruin everything for Clive.

He slid his phone back into the pocket of his suit jacket and smiled at his wife as she entered the foyer. They were due at church in fifteen minutes. His children were presenting a short Christmas production.

Murder wasn't going to get in the way of Clive's enjoyment.

Chapter Eleven

Dwight D. Eisenhower High School
Blue Island, 9:30 a.m.

The Christmas tree in the corner next to the trophy display case mocked Merri. It was Christmas and she had facilitated a break-in at a high school.

How unorthodox was that?

Her parents would be mortified.

Like many of the actions she had taken in the name of getting the job done, they didn't have to know. They were far better off not knowing. Or maybe she was the one who was better off.

The key had gotten them into the

building. Fortunately the trophy display case was not locked. All they had to do now was determine how Kick had hidden a clue in or around the trophy.

As his sister had explained, the trophy, along with newspaper clippings regarding his success and a recent photo, held a position of prominence in the display case. No wonder Kick was so proud. Everyone who visited the school's office would see that Mr. Invisible was no longer invisible in the least.

In fact, in some ways he had been too visible.

Brandon touched her on the shoulder. As usual, heat simmered in her belly. Holding her breath, she turned to him.

"There's nothing on the bottom." Brandon tapped the trophy's marble base, then turned it upright. "I'll see if it's possible to take it apart."

Merri had already checked the entire shelf, as well as the one above it, and the newspaper clippings and photo. Nothing had been written, underlined or circled. If Kick had been trying to send them a message, it wasn't in the memorabilia related to the trophy.

Merri nodded her agreement. Like Brandon, she was certain the clues led to this collection. It was only a matter of determining what it meant.

If Kick had been trying to guide them to another location, they hadn't understood.

Brandon sat down on the tiled floor with the trophy. Merri eased down into a cross-legged position next to him. The only place the trophy appeared to give was where it was screwed to the base. Her pulse began that rapid rat-a-tat-tat as Brandon removed the base.

As soon as the marble square was pulled away from the faux metal trophy, a mini storage device, a jump drive, fell to the tiled floor.

Brandon waited until Merri was looking at him and smiled. His lips formed the word, *"violà."*

Could this really be the evidence that had cost Kick his life?

"I should call Simon," Merri said.

"Let's see what's on it first," Brandon suggested.

Wouldn't hurt. Her cell phone was dead anyway. The battery had given out sometime during the night, and her stuff was at the motel. No doubt there were working phones in the school, but Brandon was right. The call could be made after they had verified the contents of the storage device.

Brandon handed her the jump drive, then carefully replaced the base on the trophy. He got to his feet and returned the trophy to its place in the display case.

Merri levered herself upward with his help. "Where can we look at this?" A high school would likely have computers.

"Come on."

She liked that he held on to her hand as they hurried down the dimly lit hall.

With few windows in the long corridor, the route was very nearly dark. They didn't dare turn on any lights for fear that someone would notice they were inside. Merri doubted that anyone else was on the premises, but neither she nor Brandon could be certain. Why take the risk?

He led her to the math department and then into the computer lab. Signs of the holiday dotted the room. A wreath on the bulletin board and relevant items in the window. Brandon pulled an extra chair in front of the monitor he'd chosen.

While he booted up the computer, Merri took the opportunity to study his profile. She wondered if there was someone special in his life. A woman who would question where he was.

It shouldn't have bothered her that a significant other was a possibility, but it did. Somehow she liked it that he was all alone except for her. That he needed her. And she needed him.

Pathetic, Merri.

Just because she felt alone didn't mean everyone else had to.

Not everyone else, she acknowledged. Him. Brandon. She liked being his saving grace.

She liked being close to him.

Maybe because he understood what it was like to be different. None of the men in her life before had understood that. Not really. Lord knew, her fiancé hadn't cared, much less understood. She and her mentor, Steven Barlow, had attempted a relationship of sorts. But he was so busy playing protector that she couldn't deal with his smothering ways.

Mason Conrad didn't really count. He'd been a distraction for Merri. A dangerous distraction. He'd turned state's evidence and gotten the charges against him dropped. He still called her from time to time, but she wasn't going down that road.

He was into the protector gig, too. He

wanted her safe. She reminded him of his sister. He'd said that to her. Merri wanted to be treated like an equal. Respected. Was that too much to ask for?

She shook off the thoughts. "What?" Brandon had spoken, but he hadn't been looking at her.

He faced her. "Sorry." He gestured to the computer screen. "Here we go."

A box opened on the screen. Brandon selected the only icon contained inside it. A larger box expanded on the screen and a video flickered into view.

Kevin Randolph's image cleared. "What you're about to see," he said, "is the statement of a man who is now dead. I copied the video to this storage device and hid it in a place only my best friend and roommate could possibly find."

Merri glanced at Brandon's profile. The hard, pained lines made her gut clench. This was more than a little difficult for him. He and Kick had been close despite their screaming matches over the rent.

Another image appeared, then cleared. This one an older man. He identified himself as a thug whose name Merri recognized from the obituaries a couple of weeks back.

She and Brandon sat, stunned, while the older gentleman cited all the infractions of those connected to Chicago's prestigious Crime Commission—including the leader, Clive Mathias. He listed case by case, infraction by infraction before closing.

When the man had completed his dissertation, Kick faded back into view.

"I've been a pain in the ass," Kick said. "But do this one thing for me, buddy. Make sure Clive Mathias doesn't get away with keeping the funds rolling to his machine with continued Mob connections."

Randolph paused a moment, then added, "Tell my family I love them. That I don't regret what I chose to do."

The screen went to black.

Brandon removed the storage device from the hard drive and tucked it into his pocket. "What now?"

Merri blinked back the tears that had brimmed in her eyes. She didn't know Kevin Randolph, but he'd worked hard to prove he was as good as anyone else. He had a family. And now he was dead.

He deserved justice. It wouldn't bring him back, but it would be a big step toward finishing what he'd started. Mathias was not going to get away with this any longer.

"We call Simon." Merri pushed to her feet. "He'll see that this evidence gets into the hands of the proper authorities. Considering this—" she gestured to the storage device "—I'm certain we'll have no trouble proving you had nothing to do with his death."

"We can use the phone in the office." Brandon was out of his seat before he'd completed the statement.

They ran to the office.

This couldn't wait.

The men tracking them could have gone to Kick's sister's house by now and figured out where they were. Merri needed Simon on this.

This part she and Brandon couldn't do alone.

"Damn it!"

The office was locked.

"Try the key," Merri urged.

The key that had allowed them access to the building wouldn't open the door to the office.

"There has to be another phone."

Brandon glanced around the corridor, then shifted his attention to her. "The cafeteria and library will be locked, as well."

Each would likely have an individual key.

"We'll have to drive to a pay phone." Merri didn't like the idea of allowing one more minute to pass without calling Simon but they had little choice.

"Wait." Brandon crossed the corridor, picked up a random chair and rushed toward the office.

Merri's jaw sagged when she realized what he planned to do. He slammed the wood chair into the glass wall of the office. It took a few tries, but the glass finally cracked, forming hundreds of veins before caving down onto itself in a pile on the floor. He tossed the damaged chair aside and grabbed her hand before treading cautiously across the broken safety glass.

"The alarm is going off," he told her. "Make the call before the police arrive."

Explaining to the authorities would steal precious time. The call had to be made before there were any interruptions.

Merri grabbed the handset from the cradle of the phone on the counter and began entering the numbers for Simon's cell phone. He wouldn't be caught without it wherever he was on this holiday.

She held her breath and counted to ten slowly, time enough for Simon to answer since she couldn't hear the rings.

Brandon's hand was suddenly on her shoulder. She glanced at him. "Put the phone down."

What the hell was he talking about? He nodded toward the door behind her. Merri turned around.

Two police officers stood in the middle of the broken glass, weapons drawn. "Hands up," one of them said.

Merri slowly placed the handset back in the cradle and did as the officer had asked.

Her heart thumped high in her chest. "Call Simon Ruhl at the Colby Agency," she demanded. "It's imperative that he come as quickly as possible."

"The chief gave orders that the two of you were to come with us," the second of the two officers commanded. "I don't know what the hell is going on, but we're to take you to Larry Stover's house."

Merri's attention flew to Brandon. What was going on here? Bethany had helped them.

"What's happened?" he demanded, fury and fear tightening his jaw.

"Bethany Stover's missing." The second officer's eyes narrowed. "And the two of you have her vehicle."

Merri's gaze met Brandon's once more.

"They've got her," he said, pain replacing the fury and fear.

Merri could think of nothing to say to reassure him.

Bethany Stover would end up as dead as her brother unless the criminals got what they wanted.

The evidence that would clear Brandon…that would ensure justice.

Chapter Twelve

Jamie, Victoria's granddaughter, had opened the last of her Christmas presents and the family was enjoying spiced cider when the doorbell rang.

Victoria's gaze sought and found Lucas's. This would not be good news.

"I'll get it." Jim was up and moving toward the front door before Victoria could voice her worries.

She prayed nothing had happened to Merri.

Victoria attempted to hold a smile in

place for her sweet grandchild. It didn't help that Tasha kept sending concerned looks Victoria's way. Lucas's stoic profile was equally troubling.

No one had been more certain than Victoria that Merri was fully capable of being a Colby Agency investigator and pursuing a case alone.

What if she had been wrong?

"Victoria."

She turned at the sound of her son's voice.

"Would you and Lucas come into the kitchen for a moment?"

"Of course."

Tasha busied her daughter with installing her new digital game player while Victoria and Lucas silently followed Jim to the kitchen.

Simon waited, his dire expression confirming Victoria's worst fears.

"Kevin Randolph's sister has been taken hostage," Simon explained, "for reasons that are still unclear. Merri and her client are at the Stover home along with the local police. Ian has already headed there. I wanted to inform you in person before I join him."

Victoria shook her head. "Good Lord, on Christmas, of all days. Doesn't this woman have small children?"

"Yes," Simon confirmed. "The local authorities won't allow any communication with Merri at this time. I'm certain when Ian arrives that will change. At this point, we can only assume that this is yet another attempt to gain access to this evidence that appears to be tied to Randolph's murder."

"Perhaps I should go," Victoria offered.

Simon shook his head. "There's no need for your involvement on that level as yet. Ian and I will handle the situation. I'll keep you informed."

"Very well. I'll expect to hear from you soon."

"Absolutely."

Jim showed Simon to the door.

Lucas put his arm around Victoria's shoulders. "Don't worry, my dear. Merri knows what she's doing. She'll have a plan in place. With Ian's and Simon's help, she can't possibly go wrong."

"If something happens to her or this missing woman," Victoria said, "the responsibility will be mine. It was my decision to move Merri forward into the field. No one else's."

"First of all," Lucas reminded her, "we both know that isn't true. Simon and numerous others, including myself, were on that same bandwagon. Secondly, I've never known you to read a potential investigator wrong. Merri's got what it takes. You made the right decision."

Victoria searched her loving husband's eyes for the confidence and determination she needed. But the truth was simple and all too straightforward.

"She's deaf, Lucas. If she goes after those men alone, she might not survive."

"Ian and Simon will never allow her to go off half-cocked like that."

"Unless she's pulled the trigger already," Victoria countered.

Merri wasn't one to waste time. If she believed the situation merited going in, she would go in.

With or without backup.

Chapter Thirteen

Chicago, 10:40 a.m.

"We have the woman."

The idea aggrieved Clive. He hated involving civilians like this. But Kick Randolph had left him no choice.

"Does the husband understand what's at stake?" Clear instructions had been given to his men; one foul-up could ruin everything.

"Yes, sir," his henchman guaranteed. "We told the husband that if he said a word beyond the script we had given him that his wife would die and his little boy would be next."

"Excellent." That would be sufficient motivation for the lowly schoolteacher to do the right thing. He wouldn't want to raise his two children alone or to risk losing one of them.

"We're waiting now for Thomas to follow through with his end."

Clive wondered how the fool intended to get past the police. But then, that wasn't his worry. Brandon Thomas would have to find a way unless he wanted to be responsible for Bethany Stover's death. He sure as hell wouldn't be welcomed into the Randolph home then.

Idiots. All of them. Kevin Randolph should have stayed out of this.

It was annoying enough that Randolph had had to be killed. This additional effort was beyond ridiculous.

"Do what you have to do," Clive instructed. "I don't want any loose ends left on this."

"I understand, sir."

Clive pressed the End Call button. In the future, he would ensure that loyalty was not an issue.

In this day, a man should be grateful for his job. That lesson needed to be driven home.

Clive had better things to do than to worry about whether his people were toeing the line. Perhaps the whole crew needed a humbling experience.

One that would remind them of what they had to lose. Of who was the boss.

Perhaps one dead reporter wasn't lesson enough.

Chapter Fourteen

Blue Island, Stover Home, 10:45 a.m.

"How many times do we have to go over this?" Brandon asked, disgusted with the cops.

The encounter had turned into a fiasco. Thank God the children weren't here to witness it. Larry's parents had come for them when this all began. The Randolphs were too distraught to be of any assistance under the circumstances.

The two men who had brought him and Merri to Bethany's house were posted outside. The chief had asked the same questions over and over.

Brandon had already passed off the storage device to Merri. He'd been right to do so. The chief had searched him the instant he'd set foot in the house. His search of Merri had been cursory at best. Wherever she'd hidden the jump drive, the chief hadn't found it. Until Brandon understood how he could help Bethany, he didn't want the evidence passed off to the police.

The front door opened and one of the officers stuck his head inside. "Chief, you've got a call I think you're going to want to take out here."

The chief grumbled but didn't argue. "I'll be right back." He glared at Brandon. "Don't either of you move."

When the chief was out the door, Larry rushed over to where Brandon stood. "I don't know what's going on," he whispered fiercely, "but they gave me this." He thrust a cell phone at Brandon. "As soon as you can get away, you're to call the one number programmed into this phone. They'll take whatever it is that you have in exchange for my Bethy." The misery in the man's eyes tore at Brandon's insides. "I don't care what you have to do, but get her back. Do you hear me?"

Brandon took the phone and nodded. "We know what they want."

Larry stepped back as the chief reentered the house.

"Any word, Chief?" Larry asked.

While the chief was distracted by Larry's question, Brandon passed the phone to Merri just in case the chief decided to search him again.

"All right." The chief turned back to Brandon. "Let's go over this one more time."

Brandon wanted to shake the man. "Chief, you don't understand—"

"I'm sorry," Merri cut in, "but I have to go to the bathroom."

The chief held up his hands. "No way

is anyone leaving this room until I know what the hell is going on."

Merri bit her bottom lip and made a pained face. "I really, really have to go."

"This isn't about her," Brandon interjected, "it's me they want."

The chief relaxed marginally. "We're finally getting somewhere." He glared at Merri. "Go. But you come right back here."

She nodded and rushed from the room.

Brandon watched her go. He had a bad feeling.

"Start at the beginning," the chief barked. "This time, don't leave anything out."

MERRI WATCHED from the hall. She waited until she was certain the men were fully involved in the conversation and then slipped into the kitchen. A laptop sat on a section of the kitchen counter obviously designated the mail and/or bill-paying station. The computer was up and running, the screen saver flashing one photo after the other of the Stover children. She pressed the Mute button and went onto the Internet server. She quickly inserted the storage device and downloaded a copy onto the desktop. When she'd finished, she sent an e-mail to Simon Ruhl's Colby Agency e-mail address with the downloaded item attached.

She stuffed the storage device into the pocket of her baggy, borrowed jeans and did the only thing she could. She sneaked out the back door and lunged across the yard in a full run. When she'd reached the back of the church where Brandon had taken her, she paused long enough to send a text message to the number programmed into the cell phone.

Ready for pickup. Hurry!

She included the location of the church. Thankfully the backdoor was no longer locked, allowing her to slip into the kitchen unnoticed by those gathered in the sanctuary for mass. She did what she knew she had to do, then she returned to the parking lot.

Undoubtedly someone had been watching the Stover home since a sedan pulled into the already crowded lot scarcely three minutes later. Christmas mass was still ongoing, but thankfully there were no parishioners in the lot. Merri strode straight to the passenger side and got in.

"Where's Thomas?" the man behind the wheel demanded.

"He's a little tied up right now," Merri explained. "I'll be taking care of this part for him."

"You got the evidence?"

"I do."

The driver wasn't pleased, but he didn't argue. He pointed the car toward the street and gave it the gas.

He glanced at Merri. "I hope you know what you're getting into."

She did.

She was about to trade herself for Bethany Stover.

"WHERE IS your friend?" the chief demanded. He walked to the hall and shouted Merri's name toward the bathroom door.

Brandon didn't wait for a response. He hurried around the chief and banged on the door. "Merri!"

Then he stopped himself. She couldn't hear him banging or calling. He twisted the knob and pushed the door inward.

The bathroom was empty.

They searched the house, the chief blubbering threats every step of the way.

Merri was gone.

In the living room once more, Brandon and Larry exchanged a look. Merri had the phone and the evidence. She had gone to do what neither of them could.

And it would likely get her killed.

Fear twisted into knots of agony in Brandon's gut.

The front door opened again.

This time the officer was accompanied by another man, this one in a dark suit and trench coat that Brandon recognized all too well.

"My name is Ian Michaels." He flashed his identification for the chief as he surveyed the room, then turned to Brandon. "Where is Merri?"

Chapter Fifteen

Blue Island Pie Factory, 12:05 p.m.

Merri raised her head up. A groan escaped her lips. She couldn't hear it, but she remembered what it sounded like. What it felt like, vibrating across her lips.

"...for yourself."

She blinked, tried to focus on the guy's lips. "What?" She'd missed part of what the bastard said.

"Just tell us where the evidence is and we'll release both you and the Stover woman."

Merri shook her head. Pain radiated through her skull. She'd been punched.

Her hair had been pulled and her head banged against the wall a couple of times. All while poor Bethany Stover watched.

"Let her go," Merri repeated, "and I'll tell you where I hid the evidence." She cringed when her swollen lip burned with the movement of her lips.

She'd hidden the jump drive at the church. They would never in a million years find it. Not that it mattered. As soon as Simon saw the video, these bastards were finished, as was their boss.

The factory they'd brought her to had been closed for years. With the car hidden behind the old loading dock, she doubted anyone searching for her and Bethany would have any luck.

Not a good thing since Merri was reasonably sure that releasing Bethany had never been on the agenda.

The assault started once more. The fiercer the tactics, the louder Bethany wailed as if she were the one absorbing the blows.

Merri's vision dimmed. She was close to passing out. She couldn't let that happen or they both would end up dead. She had to make a move. She'd endured as much for as long as possible in order to buy time.

"Okay, okay," Merri said, halting the next blow, "I'll show you where I hid it." She peered through swollen lids at the woman on the other side of the room. "But we all go together."

She held her breath while the man considered her proposal. Her heart wouldn't let her breathe again until he'd nodded and said, "Let's go."

Merri and Bethany were shoved into the backseat. Merri had approximately a dozen seconds to whisper to the woman next to her, "First chance you get, run like hell. Don't look back."

The man who appeared to be in charge slid behind the wheel while his cohort sat in the front passenger seat, carefully keeping his weapon trained on Bethany.

There were few options, so Merri went with the flow.

"At the church near the Stover home," she told the driver. "I hid it there after I escaped from the house."

The driver's eyes narrowed at her via the rearview mirror. He threw her a glance over the seat. "You better not be lying if you want to stay alive."

"You'll see," she said as he turned back to the wheel.

And he would. He would see lots of things. One more important than all the others: Merri Walters wasn't going down without a fight.

AT THE CHURCH, she instructed him to pull around back. When she'd gone inside and hidden the jump drive, the backdoor had been unlocked. She hoped like hell it still was. Mass had been over for a while and folks had gone home to enjoy the holiday with their loved ones.

The driver got out of the car and came

around to her door. He opened it, and she staggered to her feet. Her entire body ached, felt like a punching bag. With good reason—it *had* been a punching bag.

She led the way through the back door. The church was empty as she hoped. Thankfully no one had hung around after the Christmas service. The last thing she wanted was more innocent victims involved in this.

In the kitchen, she nodded to the coffeemaker. "It's in a sandwich Baggie where the coffee filter goes."

Still suspicious but ever hopeful, the gunman snatched the filter basket from the machine and grabbed the plastic bag from inside. A smile spread across his lips when he saw that it was a computer storage device capable of holding the evidentiary video.

While he removed the jump drive from the bag, Merri made her move. She seized the carafe from the warming plate and slammed it against the side of his head with all her strength before he could block her move.

She kicked him hard in the shin. The weapon in his hand fell to the floor and slid across the well-worn vinyl. Blood running down his face, he grabbed for her when she made a run for it. She barely escaped the clutch of his cruel fingers.

Another weapon! She needed another weapon. First she had to run. As soon as he had gotten the gun palmed once more, he would be after her.

She darted into the sanctuary and dove between two rows of benches. Wood splintered in the back of the bench behind her.

She blinked, understood that it was a bullet hole. He had his gun. Was after her. If she was lucky, the other guy would hear the gunshots and come inside to see what was going on. Maybe Bethany would have a chance to run.

Merri rolled beneath the bench he'd

fired at, then she kept rolling, moving toward the front door by way of the floor beneath the rows of pews.

More of those splintered holes appeared in the backs of the pews. Merri kept going, couldn't let herself be distracted. By the time she reached the final pew, the front door burst open.

The trouser legs and shoes weren't familiar to her. Not Brandon or the police—the other bad guy.

Run, Bethany, she urged with all her mental might.

Run!

"YOU'RE CERTAIN that besides the motel, this is the only place you took her?" Ian Michaels asked again.

He was as bad as the chief. "Yes," Brandon repeated.

Wait. He frowned. That wasn't entirely true. They'd spent the night in that old driveway by the abandoned house. Simon's car was still hidden there.

Would she go there?

They were almost at the church. Might as well check there first. It was well within walking distance of Bethany's home.

As if the thought had somehow summoned her, Bethany ran into the street screaming at the top of her lungs.

The car skidded to a stop, barely a foot from where she stood in shock.

The chief, Michaels, Ruhl and Brandon bailed out.

"Bethany." Brandon was the first to reach her. "Where's Merri?"

"She's—"

Before she could finish her statement shots rang out from the church.

Brandon lunged in that direction. He didn't care that he didn't have a weapon, much less a plan.

He only cared that Merri was in there and shots were being fired.

A bullet hit the door just as he reached it. He dropped on all fours onto the stoop.

With his peripheral vision, he could see that Ruhl and Michaels had fanned out around the building. The chief appeared to be calling for backup.

When the silence dragged on, Brandon reached up and grabbed the door handle. He hoisted himself up and flung the doors open.

One man was on the floor, down for the count.

The other sat astride Merri's waist, her back pinned to the floor. His weapon was bored into her forehead.

"Now you die!" the bastard roared.

"What she gave you was a fake," Brandon shouted.

The man suddenly looked up at him, the weapon still drilling a hole between Merri's eyes. "You're a little too late," he mused.

"Do you want the evidence or not?"

Brandon reached into his pocket. The man's preoccupation with whether Brandon would draw a weapon from his pocket was just the distraction Merri needed. She propelled the heel of her hand into the lower part of the gunman's chin. His head snapped back. The weapon fired, hitting the floor right next to her head.

Brandon rushed forward, kicked the guy in the skull.

The gunman tumbled off Merri.

She rolled away and grabbed a weapon lying a few feet away. Apparently, it was the other man's gun.

When she'd gotten to her feet, gun held expertly in her hands, she snarled, "Merry Christmas!" She kicked the gunman in the head again before he could get up.

The chief, Michaels and Ruhl rushed into the sanctuary.

Brandon pulled Merri into his arms and held her tight against his chest.

He was so glad she was safe.

He'd realized a few hours ago that his life would be immensely sad without her.

All he had to do was convince her that he was worth the trouble of getting to know.

Maybe that would take a while.

But he had plenty of time.

Chapter Sixteen

Chicago Police Department, 4:00 p.m.

Brandon had been here for two hours.

The police had taken both men from the church into custody.

The district attorney was reviewing the evidence Brandon had given him.

All good. Except that Merri was in the hospital and this crap was keeping Brandon from going to see her.

He wanted out of here.

"Mr. Thomas." Detective Morales, Whitehall's replacement on the case, entered the room. "You may go home now. You're a free man."

Brandon didn't remind him that he didn't actually have a home at the moment.

"Thank you." He hesitated before walking out the door of the interview room. "Does the D.A. have enough evidence to take down Mathias?"

That was what mattered to Brandon. The guy responsible for Kick's death should pay.

Morales smiled. "That and more."

Brandon was satisfied. He walked out of the interrogation room, down the long corridor and out of the building.

He had no idea where he'd left his car last. A taxi would do just fine. Anything to get to Merri.

A dark sedan rolled up in front of him. "You need a lift, Mr. Thomas?"

Ian Michaels.

"I want to see Merri," he said, making no bones about it. Brandon wasn't so sure this guy liked him, but right now he didn't care. He just wanted to get to Merri.

"Headed that way," Michaels agreed.

From the precinct, it took ten minutes to reach Mercy General.

When Brandon got out, he was surprised that Michaels didn't do the same.

"I've already checked in on her," Michaels told him. "She wants to see you." Michaels allowed the corners of his mouth to tilt into a smile. "That says a hell of a lot about you, Thomas. I hope you won't make her regret her faith in you."

Ian Michaels drove away then. It was just as well, because Brandon had no idea how to respond to the man.

Of course he wouldn't make Merri regret wanting to see him. Would he?

He was willing to take the risk. As long as she was.

As Brandon rode the elevator up to her floor, he considered that the D.A. had agreed to allow one of Kick's friends to have an exclusive on the breaking Mathias story as long as Kick got the byline. The *Trib* was willing to do whatever necessary to get the story of the decade.

Chicago's Crime Commissioner Goes Down for Dirty Deeds.

Merri's door was closed. Brandon started to knock but remembered that she wouldn't hear him so he pushed the door inward one slow inch at a time.

When she didn't object, he came into the room and sat down beside her bed. She was sleeping, he realized, and he let her be. He got comfortable in the chair next to her bed and closed his eyes. He couldn't remember when he'd slept more than a couple of hours. Before Kick's murder, he supposed.

Cool fingers touched his face, traced a path along his jaw.

His eyes fluttered open and he smiled. "You're awake. How do you feel?"

"Like hell."

He stood next to her bed so he could look at her and hold her hand. "You look like hell."

"Thanks. You really know how to sweet-talk a girl." She tried to smile, but then touched her bruised and broken lips. "They won't let me go home."

"When the tests are finished you can go," he promised. She didn't have any head injuries, contusions or concussions. But there were possibly a couple of cracked ribs and other bumps and bruises. She would be checked thoroughly before being released. "You may even have to stay the night." Michaels had mentioned that on the way over here.

"No way am I spending Christmas night in here," she argued. "I'd rather be home."

He inspected her fingers one by one. "I'll stay with you. That is, if you want me to."

"It'll be boring."

"I don't care."

"I'm pretty cranky."

"What's new?" he teased.

"Here you are asking me to stay the night," she said softly, "and you haven't even kissed me."

"I think I can remedy that." Brandon leaned down and gently brushed his lips across her cheek. That was the most he dared with her all banged up.

She arched an eyebrow at him. "If that's the best you can do, we've got trouble."

He stared at her lips, wanted nothing more than to taste those sweet, bruised lips. "If you're sure."

She grabbed him by the shirt front and pulled him down to her. "Kiss me, damn it."

He kissed her, softly, on the lips. She made a sound that sent an ache through him. The taste of her was addictive.

When he pulled his lips from hers, he swept the hair from her cheek with his fingertips. "We make quite the pair."

She took his hand in hers and kissed his palm, then winced.

He grimaced.

"We're two of a kind," she agreed. "I think tonight will be the first night of many."

"But I don't have a Christmas gift for you." He'd scarcely had time to think about the holiday.

Another of those wicked grins tugged at her battered lips. "Yes you do and I can't wait to open it."

"We'll open it together," he murmured before brushing a kiss to the tip of her nose, about the only part of her face that wasn't bruised and battered.

"Merry Christmas, Brandon." She stared deeply into his eyes. "This is the best Christmas ever."

"Ditto."

He sealed their sweet words with more kisses. He lightly touched his lips to every place that bastard had damaged. But mostly, he just wanted to touch her with his fingers…his mouth…and too many other parts to mention.

She was right. This was the best Christmas ever.

Chapter Seventeen

"A toast." Victoria held her glass high. When her entire staff had reciprocated, she said, "To all of us. May our New Year be filled with beauty and wonder and, most of all, peace."

The clinking of glasses and the murmurs of agreement went around the room.

Merri didn't have to hear the words and cheers; she remembered what they sounded like. She drank deeply of her champagne, then stared into the dark eyes of the man at her side. Her bruises were clearing up. The swelling was gone and she wasn't sore anymore.

Kick Randolph's story had seized attention all across the nation. His family was so proud. The mayor of Blue Island had even named a day in his honor.

Work at the Colby Agency was as steady as always. The prospects for the New Year were all favorable.

Merri was considering asking Brandon to move into her place with her. He'd been living in a hotel for the past week. They'd spent every possible moment together. They might as well live together.

Maybe in a couple of months she would take him down to Nashville to meet her parents. They would love him.

She, though she'd scarcely known him more than a week, was pretty sure she was in love with him.

Time would tell.

And between now and then, they

would live life to the fullest. Not regretting, not looking back. Only forward.

Her cell phone vibrated in the glittery little purse hanging from her wrist.

She couldn't imagine who it was. Her family had already called and wished her a happy New Year. Steven had sent her a text, to which she did not respond. She wasn't giving him reason to hang on. They were over. He needed to get on with his life just as she had.

Tugging the phone from the small bag, she slid it open and viewed the incoming call.

Mason Conrad.

A shock rattled her.

Hadn't she made herself clear yet?

She couldn't hear herself think out here, so she ducked into the nearest office and answered the call.

"Walters."

She read the words he uttered as they filled the screen on her cell. "Merri. It's good to hear your voice."

She frowned. "Happy New Year, Mason, but I'm right in the middle of a party. I should let you go."

She watched as more of his words spilled across the screen. "Wait. We never talk anymore. Why don't I come up there and we'll spend some quality time together."

Oh, no. She'd fallen for that one before.

"The truth is," she said frankly, "I've found someone, Mason. I don't want you to call me anymore."

She stared at the blank screen in anticipation of his words.

"For real this time?"

He was referring to the doomed relationship she'd had with Steven.

"Yes, Mason. For real this time. I love this guy. As a matter of fact—" she screwed up her courage "—I think I'm going to marry this one. I've known since the first night we met that he was special."

"Great," he finally said, the word appearing on the screen with all the flatness she felt certain he'd said it.

"Yes, it is great. I love my job. I love my life. And I love the man. So just back off." The phone was abruptly lifted from her fingers. She looked up to find Brandon standing close behind her.

"You should listen to her, dude," Brandon warned. "We're together now and nothing else matters." Brandon pushed the End Call button and set her phone on the nearest surface. "Now—" he pulled her into his arms "—that's the first time I've heard you say you love me."

"I guess I was just a little afraid that it might be like a fleeting spell or something. You know, like Christmas magic."

"And what did you conclude?"

"That this is real." She kissed his chin. "And that we complete each other somehow."

"And," he said rubbing of his nose

against hers, "that this is not only a new year, but a new beginning for us."

Forever.

The word echoed in her mind as his lips closed over hers.

This was the real thing.

And it was finally Merri's.

* * * * *

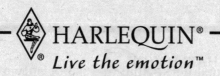

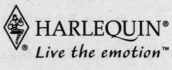

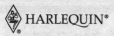

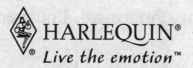

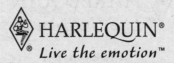

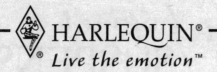

Love Inspired® SUSPENSE
RIVETING INSPIRATIONAL ROMANCE

These contemporary tales
of intrigue and romance
feature Christian characters
facing challenges to their faith...
and their lives!

**Four new Love Inspired Suspense titles are
available every month wherever books are
sold, including most bookstores, supermarkets,
drug stores and discount stores.**

Steeple
Hill®

Visit:
www.steeplehillbooks.com